Machine Art and
Other Writings

Essays selected and edited, and with an introduction

by Maria Luisa Ardizzone

Duke University Press   Durham & London 1996

Machine Art and Other Writings

The Lost Thought of the Italian Years

Ezra Pound

For every thinking
which is lost.

Contents

Acknowledgments

This book contains a selection of Ezra Pound's unpublished prose (along with two rare texts) written during the years he lived in Italy (Rapallo and Venice), specifically from 1927 to the early 1940s. In and of themselves, these writings are of considerable interest and contain rich source material for our understanding of the poet's developing views on economics, metaphysics, and poetics. This volume offers us a new understanding of Pound's middle years. As shown in the introduction, my method of reading has been governed by Pound's proposal, at the end of the 1920s, of his criticism as a method of reading in the planned edition of *Collected Prose*. My point in collecting these writings focuses on a conception of aesthetics (I have indicated it as an aesthetics of *technê*) which is basic to a reading of Pound's Cantos written from 1945 on, and mostly to the sections *Rock-Drill* and *Thrones*. My forthcoming book, *Ezra Pound: Il Paradiso* (*Ezra Pound: The Paradise*), will contain more on this topic in its relationship to Pound's late *Cantos*.

Most of the research for this book was made possible by three awards: two fellowships from the Consiglio Nazionale delle Ricerche of Italy (CNR), 1989–1990 and 1990–1991, and one from Montedison Progetto Cultura in 1986. Some texts collected here and bits of my introduction appeared in my *Ezra Pound e la Scienza* (Milano: Scheiwiller, 1987); in "Some Additions and Corrections to *Ezra Pound e la scienza*," ed. Jacqueline Key, *Ezra Pound and America* (London: Macmillan, 1992), 3–18; in my article "Pound's Language in *Rock-Drill:* Two Theses for a Genealogy," *Paideuma* (Winter 1992): 121–148; and in "The Genesis and Structure of Pound's Paradise: Looking at the Vocabulary," *Paideuma*, (season, 1996): 121–148.

I owe the strongest debt of gratitude to Mary de Rachewiltz, first for a long intellectual instigation, and then for reading this book at its various stages, for her generous guarantee of access to Pound's library in Brunnenburg, her advice, and for more than I can say. I am deeply indebted to Vanni Scheiwiller for having introduced me to Pound a long time ago, for many kinds of generosity and assistance he has given me over many years.

Other debts are to Professor Donald Gallup, for his encouragement and exacting scrutiny during my research periods in the Beinecke Library, Yale University. I also want to thank James Laughlin IV and Professor A. Walton Litz.

I am grateful to the Director of Beinecke Library, Ralph Franklin, and to Patricia Willis, Curator of the American Collection of the Beinecke Library; and to Willard Goodwin of Harry Ransom Humanities Research Center, University of Texas, Austin. I am grateful to Professor John Farge of the Pontifical Institute of Medieval Studies in Toronto for kind hospitality at the Institute during the fall semester of 1992, and to Professor Timothy Reiss of New York University's Department of Comparative Literature, for a long conversation that led me to rethink passages of my introduction. I am also grateful to Professor Reiss for having invited me to the Comparative Literature Department as a Visiting Scholar in the spring semester of 1993, thanks to which I have been able to complete this manuscript. I would like to express my gratitude to Professor Maria Corti of the University of Pavia for important advice on the organization of this volume and for various illuminating conversations; and to Professor Giuseppe Billanovich of the Universitá Cattolica in Milan for his comments on *Pound e la scienza* and for his generous assistance in my own research at the Universitá Cattolica. I am also highly indebted to my Italian friends: Franca Ghitti for her mastery in art and in art as *technê*, and Guglielmo Castagnetti for having shared with me for many years his knowledge of philosophy and his library. I am grateful to Professor Tim Redman for reading the manuscript and for his suggestions.

The staffs of many libraries have contributed their facilities and time. I have first of all to thank that of the Beinecke Library, particularly Steve Jones, and of Harry Ransom Humanities Center, the Universitá Cattolica in Milan and Brescia, the Library of the Pontifical Institute of

Medieval Studies, and the libraries of the University of Rochester and of New York University.

I am also grateful to my former student at the University of Rochester, Patrick Pullano, for typing and retyping the manuscript, and for his patience in assisting me; to Peter Kalkavage, for editorial assistance and for translating fragments of my introduction written in Italian; and to Christopher Winks, a graduate student in Comparative Literature at New York University, for helping me in the final stages of this project.

The manuscript of this book was completed in June 1993. However, the final revision of the text would have been impossible without the atmosphere of intellectual debate with my colleagues in the Italian Department of New York University, directed by John Freccero.

Maria Luisa Ardizzone
New York

Abbreviations

BRBL   New Haven, Connecticut, Beinecke Rare Book Manuscript, Yale University, Pound Archive

HRHR   Austin, Texas, Harry Ransom Humanities Research Center, University of Texas

The abbreviation (PB) indicates Pound's personal books that are preserved in Brunnenburg, Italy.

For *The Cantos,* references are to the 1970 New Directions edition.

"[their] best form comes from the mathematic
  of strains."—*Machine Art*

"mathematics,   the writing
  arithmetic
  algebraic
  geometric
  analytic."
  —*Pragmatic Aesthetics of E.P.*

"1/2 research   and 1/2 *Technê*
  1/2 observation,   1/2 *Technê*
  1/2 training   1/2 *Technê*
                          Tch'eng T'ang for guide."

  —*Rock-Drill 85*

abstract.

Ferdl

Bruhl.

H.T.R   1.

adv.   mimic.
        laut bilder.

gain → loss → replenish.

Introduction

Reading Rejects: A Method of Reading

The writings collected in this volume are unpublished, with the exception of two rare ones. The unpublished ones are from the Pound archives preserved in the Beinecke Rare Book and Manuscripts Library at Yale University; the rare ones are from journals.

The writings, which are ordered and divided into four sections — *Machine Art* (1927–1930), *How to Write* (1930–1936), *European Paideuma* (1940), and *Pragmatic Aesthetics of E.P.* (1940–1943)[1] — have the common characteristic of being rejected texts. Some were rejected by the editors to whom Pound submitted them, and even Pound himself indirectly rejected others, either by rewriting them, condensing them in another form, or apparently forgetting about them and leaving them unfinished. Rejected by editors of Pound anthologies and consequently by scholars who to this day have preferred to consult and use them rather than anthologize them, these texts put their editor in the position of a reader of rejects.

Machine Art is in this sense exemplary. It was rejected by Pound when in the *The New Review* (1931–1932) he inserted fifteen photographs into a brief text.[2] Previously rejected by the Chicago publishing firm Covici[3] and even excluded from the volume *Ezra Pound and the Visual Arts* (1980), it was included in *Pound e la scienza: Scritti inediti o rari* (1987).[4] Similarly, the radio broadcast "The Organum According to Tsze sze" (1942) was not included in the volume of broadcasts *Ezra Pound Speaking* (1978).[5] *European Paideuma* (1940) met objections from D. C. Fox and was not published. *Convenit esse deos* appears unfinished, as is the case with *Pragmatic Aesthetics*.

The unfinished *How to Write* (1930), in contrast, appears to be a document that Pound himself indirectly rejected. The text appears to have been written when the scheduled twelve-volume edition of *Collected Prose,* which was to have collected the poet's critical work, fell through.[6] Pound had intended the writing to be a synthesis of the essential points of his poetics. But the *ABC of Reading* (1934),[7] which supersedes this text through its extreme concentration on the same topics, represents an implicit rejection of the earlier work in that it appears to resolve upon the ideogrammic method introduced there, which in *How to Write* was put forth as still problematic.

The fragments collected here in the *Addenda* derive for the most part from the *Collected Prose* edition's failure to appear. And since Pound drew up many of them at the end of the 1920s with the intention of connecting the various sections within a large-scale collection, both *How to Write* and these fragments document a line of thought that guided Pound in the years in which he was considering publication of his critical opus as an organic whole. One demand, that of organicity, would become essential from the second half of the 1920s onward, its decisive moment being the definition in *ABC of Reading* (1934) of the ideogrammic or scientific method (whose significance, however, takes on its stratified complexity when seen in the light of *How to Write* and the *Addenda*). This organicity, to which, after the failure of the *Collected Prose,* is owed the publication of *Make it New* (1934), *ABC of Reading* (1934), and *Guide to Kulchur* (1938), is in reality, even when taken solely in relation to the Poundian vocabulary, the focal point already present in Imagism. It is revealed in the term "complex,"[8] whose origin has been tirelessly sought after by many scholars. Nevertheless, whether the term comes from psychology or from another field, the term already suggests the idea of an organic unity that the section *How to Write* will put forth, emphasizing the word "relation."

Reading Pound's Marginalia

With respect to the texts mentioned, the present volume, which contains texts written between the 1920s and the early part of the 1940s, is presented as a parallel and complementary route. My intention in publishing them is not that of the philologist who publishes texts that can be generically useful to scholars. By "philology" here I include the

meaning given to it by the Italian philosopher Giambattista Vico (1668–
1744), who plays a role in Pound's encyclopaedia: philology as the "science of the certain,"[9] where certainty here is proposed as having as its
aim a further knowledge of what is documented. The fragments—notes
included as texts in this collection—have a value which integrates that
of already known texts. Their value is fundamental in the sense that, if
something could emerge on the road to "certain knowledge" in Pound's
studies, it will come from the considering of marginal texts.

What remains is to illustrate the method with which these texts have
been read. The problems they present impose on us the need to seek
verification outside the texts themselves. This verification was provided
by the books Pound owned and read during these years. In attempting to reconstruct a reading chronology as documented by the Pound
library (Brunnenburg, Italy, and Austin, Texas)[10] and at the same time
by searching the texts for reading marks, brief glosses, and underlin-
ings, we find a continuity of thought that serves as a basis for inter-
preting the rejected work collected here. Such a methodology proves
not only useful but necessary. The comparison takes its point of departure from indications furnished by the texts; it then is expanded to yield
a fundamental thesis that can be formulated as follows. At the end of
the 1920s the polemic against abstraction, entered into by the Pound of
Imagism,[11] Vorticism,[12] and the editing of Fenollosa (*The Chinese Written Character as a Medium for Poetry* [1920]),[13] assumes new and complex proportions. Such proportions are indicated by the line of research
affirmed by the writings collected here and compared with the margi-
nalia in several volumes in Pound's library. Through such comparison,
the polemic against abstraction appears at the center of a complex and
coherent inquiry that compels us to redefine the polemic through what
is here indicated as the attempt to focus on the problem of metaphysics.
Through such redefinition (attributable not to Pound but to the editor
of the present volume), what is used is not so much Pound's terminology (the term "metaphysics" comes up only twice),[14] but contents
provided by several texts that Pound read synchronically. These texts
are fundamental to European culture, and their common point was the
refutation of Aristotelian and Scholastic metaphysics. In concentrating
on this problem, Pound appears to counter metaphysics by delineating
the sphere of aesthetics and entrusting to it the solution of the problem.

The present volume thus documents an inquiry that is continuously affirmed from *Machine Art* to *Pragmatic Aesthetics*, an inquiry in which the content and meaning of the term "aesthetics" come to be rethought.

The Criticism of Metaphysics

In the second half of the 1920s, Pound was concentrating on the *Cantos*. Insofar as the poem was epic and historical, it connoted at one of its levels the epic as the battle against the persisting metaphysics of the West. The historical aim (telos) appeared to be organized around Pound's simultaneously focusing on and removing the problem of evil in history. In Canto 45 this evil will be identified with usury, which in some of the writings collected here is placed in relation to metaphysics. Thus, one of the centers for our comprehension of these texts is located outside the texts themselves and is based on Pound's reading of Aristotle's *Metaphysics*. The reading marks, brief glosses, and the fact that Pound returned to this work on two different occasions—all of these signal a crucial point of reflection in Pound's thought.[15]

This reflection runs synchronously with the same dates on which Pound was writing and then correcting the first of the texts collected here, *Machine Art* (1927–1930), just as the return to Aristotle in the early 1940s was synchronous with the further texts collected here—*European Paideuma, Convenit esse Deos, Confucianum Organum, Pragmatic Aesthetics*—which belong to the end of the 1930s and the early 1940s. The years of Pound's greatest adherence to Fascism and of his most virulent anti-Semitic polemics are also the ones in which he once again takes up Aristotle's *Metaphysics*. Tim Redman, who in *Ezra Pound and Italian Fascism* (1991) informs us that the poet's correspondence with the Fascist politician Nino Sammartano in the early forties contains discussions of several key words in the Aristotelian *Metaphysics*, confirms the line of reading that derives from these texts.[16]

According to the evidence of the texts, the transition from the polemic against abstraction to the polemic against metaphysics occurs in the second half of the 1920s. During those years, Pound, while working on the medieval Italian poet Guido Cavalcanti, began to search for the sources of *Donna me prega* in some Aristotelian texts.[17] In reading Aristotle's work, he isolated what seemed to him the living and positive part of Aristotle's thought, while rejecting what seemed to him not only negative in itself but also pregnant with dire consequences for the history of the West. In his analysis, the positive part of Aristotelian philosophy was identified essentially with the Aristotelianism on which the Cavalcanti of *Donna me prega* had drawn, that is, a philosophy bound to Aristotelian physics and to the science of the soul as part of physics. Cavalcanti had treated love as an accident. Love was thus something appropriate to the world of physics and hence could be disengaged from the metaphysical world of the immobile substance. Now the Averroism of Cavalcanti, which Pound held in high esteem, is bound to Aristotelian physics (which Averroism underlines), to the sphere of sensibility as the perfection of body rather than to the division between sense and intellect.[18] The point of this digression is to emphasize that Pound poses the problem of metaphysics first of all as an inquiry into the neutralizing of Aristotelian physics, precisely that physics which Pound sees as living in Cavalcanti's poetry. As is well known, according to Pound this neutralizing had taken form in Aquinas's rereading and systematizing of Aristotelian thought, in which Dante too was implicated. Here, we have an aspect of Pound's thinking that is especially evident in his studies of Cavalcanti and that brings to light an early core of Pound's problem of metaphysics.

But it is evident from the texts published here that the problem of metaphysics goes well beyond Pound's study of Cavalcanti. Starting out from his commitment to the war on abstraction along with the Cavalcanti study, Pound begins to organize the problem of abstraction historically, which was transformed through being constituted as the fulcrum of absolute meditation. In those same years in which the poet was trying to identify what he defined as the problem of "evil" in "history,"[19] while it was revealing itself as usury, he made a gesture of the utmost significance when he inserted his English translation of *Donna me prega* into his *Cantos* (Canto 36). In light of these rejected manuscripts, the interpolation into the *Cantos* of the poetry of the natural philosopher Cavalcanti is seen to perform the function of opposing metaphysics, a metaphysics which on the evidence of the writings collected in this volume appears to be bound to Pound's notion of usury.

Machine Art and Other Writings allows us to identify the centrality of the problem and the resources on which Pound drew in opposing himself to the persistent metaphysics. The various texts collected here are like the tiles of a complex but coherent mosaic. The link essential to this

new awareness lies in the more robust sense of history that the draft of
the poem displayed and by means of which the problem of abstraction
is transformed into the focal point of the metaphysics conditioning the
history of the West.

This historical sense leads Pound to locate in the culture of the
Renaissance the essential turning point at which European culture was
organizing a profound critique of metaphysics. According to Pound, this
was an only partially realized project, one in which there appeared to
be a lack. With the advent of the Renaissance, a deep void opened that
was in large part responsible for the enduring metaphysics of the West.
Although critical of metaphysics, the Renaissance had not brought language up to date in light of the new science of nature. Pound's modernism thus comes before us as the consciousness of a task matured
and motivated by a historical necessity.[20] He points to language, taking
up once more and updating a revolutionary process similar in importance to that of Francis Bacon (*How to Write*). Pound's thesis assumes
the form of a diagnosis. The language of medieval culture had been a
language of precision, whereas that of modernity is not. We moderns,
according to Pound, still use a language appropriate to a medieval culture ruled by metaphysical needs.[21] With this diagnosis in mind, Pound
turns to the sphere of poetry as the locus of correction. *How to Write*
is thus a treatise that detaches poetics from rhetoric and severs its connection with the two medieval arts to which it traditionally had been
bound: grammar and dialectic.[22] *How to Write* seeks to reinstate the significance and value of writing in cognitive terms, where the concept of
beautiful style—style and metaphor as ornaments—is rejected. On the
contrary, *How to Write* postulates that writing be bound to the science
of matter, which has its place in the laboratory of the scientist, and that
this material science form the basis for the renovation of language.

The present volume is placed in a continuous relation with the essays
of the 1910s devoted to the Renaissance.[23] It reveals the binary relation that ties Pound to the culture of the Renaissance, in which he sees
the formulation of a modernity for which, starting from the *ur-Cantos*
(1917), he tries to construct the language.[24] Aware of the significance of
Renaissance culture, while at the same time critical of it, he goes over
its tracks in order to establish its contribution. For Pound, this contribution is owing not to those involved in literature, which lapsed into
rhetoric,[25] but to those who, in their effort to reject medieval culture,

had constructed the focus of the criticism of metaphysics. The crucial names that emerge from these documents initiate a Renaissance line that is not coincident with the culture of the first half of the sixteenth century. The names are: Francis Bacon (1561–1626), G. W. Leibniz (1646–1716), and G. B. Vico (1668–1744). These three names, once verified not only by what Pound writes about them but also on the basis of how he reads them (Vico, for instance, briefly recalled in *How to Write*, appears to be a crucial point of reference in *Pragmatic Aesthetics*), allow us to distinguish four aspects of Pound's critique of metaphysics in continuity with Renaissance culture: (1) the critique of the concept of form; (2) the opposition of the science of nature to the science of metaphysics; (3) the critique of the concept of substance as one and immobile and the opposition of monad as a unity both plural and relational; and (4) the critique of theoretical knowledge and the proposal of a knowing that is coincident with making.

At the top presides Bacon, next Leibniz, and then Vico as he appears in Pound's reading of the Vichian Studies of the Italian philosopher Giovanni Gentile.[26] *How to Write* puts the twentieth century in a continuity with the Renaissance. It develops the foundational project of extending the gnoseological premises of the Renaissance to language. Modernism here emerges both in opposition to and in continuity with the modern age, that is, with the culture that takes shape in Europe with humanism and the Renaissance.

This new awareness finds Pound in the act of turning the page of the history of Western culture. He comes to fill the gaps left by the culture of the Renaissance. The critique of Aristotelian logic and the substitution of the science of nature for the science of metaphysics were precisely what Bacon's *Novum Organum* had called for. *How to Write* proclaims a revolution of similar importance: the elevation of language to the level of the new knowledge embodied in the modern science of nature.

Once this line of thought is grasped, the volumes in Pound's library confirm that the fragments collected here are the documentation of an organicity. Besides Aristotle's *Metaphysics*, the other volumes are placed in perspective by this organicity, in the sense that they indicate the path toward the critique of metaphysics. The first major text is thus Bacon's *Novum Organum*, which Pound read in the Rapallo years, as indicated in the same volume.[27] The second is Leibniz's *New Essays on Human Understanding*,[28] which Pound read probably in the same period (the end of the twenties) in a French edition. And the third is Gentile's *Studi vichiani*, also probably read at the end of the 1920s and in the 1940s as well.[29] From the reading marks in these three texts, a line of thought emerges through which Pound tried to oppose metaphysics.

To be sure, Bacon[30] is valued by Pound insofar as the heart of the *Novum Organum* is the polemic against the syllogism and the replacement of the science of metaphysics by the new science of nature and the inductive method as its new instrument ("The Organum According to Tsze sze"). But more important to the ends of aesthetics is the use which Pound makes of the Baconian concept of form, without, however, referring to Bacon explicitly. Pound uses this concept to alter the reigning concept of beauty. As Bacon, he opposes the form of contemplation with the form as law, but brings this opposition into the field of aesthetics. In traditional aesthetics, Pound had located a residue of metaphysics, while putting forth the view that beauty is no longer to be regarded as an essence culled from the act of gazing, but a thing's inner law (*Machine Art*).

Leibniz is of value to Pound not only for his chapter on language in the *New Essays* but for his critique of the concept of substance.[31] *How to Write* suggests that it was probably from Leibniz's concept of organic and plural monad that Pound derived the method of "comparison" embodied in "the ideogrammic method or the method of science" (*The ABC of Reading*).[32] Knowledge is not abstraction in the sense of reduction but a combinatorial activity. Thinking is the fruit of such activity (*How to Write*).[33] The Paideuma of Frobenius had embodied the thesis that culture was an organically interrelated whole.[34] Pound seems to read Frobenius in light of Leibniz, evaluating the Leibnizian sources of Frobenius's organic concept of culture. *European Paideuma* demonstrates that the organic conception of culture—as we shall see—is one of the reasons for Pound's anti-Semitic obsession.

As we can see from his library, Pound had read an essay on Vico by Gentile. But the reading marks attest that the crux was always the repudiation of metaphysics. Pound recopies one of Vico's fundamental maxims on the title page, *intelligentia et opus unum idemque sunt*,[35] that is, "we know what we make," or, according to Vico, *verum et factum convertuntur* (a true [verum] knowledge is just that of things we have made [factum]). But in Gentile's reconstruction, Vico had limited the possibility of knowledge to history, thereby regarding as metaphysical the idea that man can know the inner process of nature.[36] Pound, in contrast with Vico, considers that science can indeed know nature and that, for this reason, the true in writing is constituted as language ruled by the mathematical laws that preside in nature (*Pragmatic Aesthetics*) and by a logic revealed by the science of matter. Logic becomes biological (*Addenda*, 14). But such biology which includes a reflection that Rémy de Gourmont[37] opened to Pound, goes well beyond Rémy de Gourmont to include biology as it is based on the new science of matter (*How to Write*). It is on the basis of this new science of matter that Pound repudiates not only the syllogism but the entire cognitive process defined by him as abstract, as a process that reduces the manifold of experience through a general abstraction.

On the surface, *Machine Art* goes into the general emphasis on the machine of those years. But in reality it signals the emergence of an independent line of thinking. Although the word *technê* does not appear in *Machine Art*, Pound's essay appears to be written in light of Aristotle's idea of art as *technê*.[38] *Technê* implies that art is not an object but a rational activity of making,[39] and at the same time *technê* takes into account the kind of knowledges which make this activity possible. It implies the concept of art as a set of rules. The category of *technê*, as identified in *Machine Art*, is the new aesthetic dimension which destroys the idea of art as imitation, all the psychologisms inherent in the idea of beauty, and the idea of style as ornament. *Machine Art* also proposes for consideration that the concept of art as *technê* thus presides over Poundian poetics starting with "How to Read" (1929).[40] "How to Write" sets forth the theoretical modes of this poetics, focusing on the problem of written language, which disclose more than can be discerned from *ABC of Reading*. The relationship between language and the science of matter that "How to Write" imposes suggests at the same time that "logopoeia,"[41] the making of the word, implies the charging of language with a meaning[42] that comes from a knowledge gained in the scientist's laboratory. This relation of writing to the science of matter is one of the levels at which the rejection of metaphysics is developed.

Language and Metaphysics

After *Machine Art*, it is from "How to Write" onward that Pound develops the pivot of his critique of metaphysics, basing his criticism on analysis of written language. The writing of the 1930s presupposes Pound's further reflections on Fenollosa's essay "The Chinese Written Character," primarily evaluating its fundamental sources. Aristotle is seen as a term to be opposed and Leibniz[43] as the means of articulating this opposition. Leibniz's monad, for Pound a unity which includes plurality and movement, opposes the Aristotelian substance of metaphysics, which is one and immobile. "Addenda" follows this line of reflection and gives us the solutions that Pound is looking for. Because he sees in the Aristotelian syllogism a reductive logic dominated by the oneness of Aristotelian substance, he opposes it with the manifold inasmuch as the latter can be derived from a logic ruled by the laws of nature. Pound uses here the term "biology," including in it the new concept of nature gained from the scientist's laboratory. Comparing the plural relations spread by the language of primitive people with the plural relations revealed by the science of matter, Pound rejects grammar insofar as it is related to syllogism; he looks for a new language that—in light of Addenda—we may indicate is taught in terms of a grammar of biology. During the same period Pound begins to evaluate certain kinds of communication employed by so-called primitive peoples: drum telegraph and Morse alphabet, which communicate without using words, and musical languages. Chinese language and primitive languages, both structured on plural relations, lead Pound to evaluate the relationship between language and culture. Pound is attempting to see if they interact. That is why, as he puts it, the so-called naturfolkers, while they possess a language of things and do not use the language of grammar and syllogism, also do not practice usury. (See letter from Pound to Fox in Appendix to this volume.)

This analysis leads Pound at the end of the 1930s to posit a further set of relationships, that is, he connects language and logic to Aristotelian monotheism and this monotheism with Judaic monotheism. While this connection serves to clarify the meaning of Pound's problem of metaphysics, at the same time it also confirms once more the interaction of the aesthetic field with the refutation of metaphysics, as that interaction takes place from the end of the 1920s.

In the second half of the 1930s, Pound's library bears witness to his reading of Aristotle's *Metaphysics* in the Greek-English Loeb edition (Books 10–14).[44] His reading marks inform us that his attention was focused on Aristotle's single immobile substance. Since the edition is that of 1935, it indicates that the return to the *Metaphysics* was oriented toward the problem already delineated in the section "How to Write" — which Pound attempted to resolve by setting the plural relations against the One, movement against immobility — a problem language had been called upon to concretize. What some of these writings propose for our consideration is the linking of this reflection to the critique of Jewish monotheism that occurs at the end of the 1930s. Pound identifies Aristotelian monotheism with Jewish monotheism, and to Jewish monotheism he attributes the responsibility for the Aristotelian monotheism. What happens in these years is that, while the *Cantos* posed the problem of locating evil in history, Pound was at the same time identifying evil as metaphysics and, without actually using this word, was showing its manifestations. At one and the same time, abstraction is the method of metaphysics and of syllogism. In the meaning Pound gives it, abstraction signifies the estrangement from nature, the reduction of the plurality to the one (to abstract means also to reduce). This idea that nature is manyness and abundance presides, at the end of the 1930s, over Pound's polemic against Aristotelian metaphysics and Semitism.

European Paideuma: **Metaphysics and Anti-Semitism**

Paideuma,[45] a term coined by the German ethnologist Leo Frobenius, implies the idea of culture as gestalt, that is, a living organism in which every component is influenced by the others. In the section *European Paideuma*, the important relation Pound proposes is the one among religion, thinking, and language. The cause of the metaphysical essence of Western culture is located in monotheism, which Pound holds responsible for abstraction as the reduction of the plurality of nature to the One. Pound attributes to the Jews the responsibility for monotheism in history, a monotheism which, having passed from Judaism into the metaphysics of Aristotle, became the basis of the mental structure of the West and of its Paideuma (*Convenit esse Deos*). The important relation here is that between language and thinking and between thinking and religion. To religion, Pound attributes the responsibility for our mental structure. The suggested relation singles out a correspondence between a religion, which tends to reduce the manifold to the monos (One), and the economic forms (usury) organized by a culture that manifests itself as reduction. Just as monotheism forms the basis of a way of thinking that tends to reduce the plural to the one, so too must it be held responsible for the economic manifestation of a culture in the form of usury, the sign of which is in language that reveals itself as the document of a culture.

In *Convenit esse Deos*, monotheism and monism[46] identified and placed in relation to logic and language, indicate that Pound's polemic against abstraction had become the fulcrum for vast and more inclusive meditation. The contemporaneous return to the *Metaphysics* of Aristotle, which Pound rereads and glosses in the early forties, confirms that such reflection is aimed at focusing on the problem of metaphysics as forming the structural basis for the culture of the West.

Pound's refutation of metaphysics includes different levels of a vast polemic whose pivot is his substantially metaphysical attitude of attributing perfection to everything that is not distanced from nature. In the Poundian reconstruction, metaphysics has its roots in the betrayal of the laws of nature, inasmuch as nature, as a generating activity, is in itself plural. For this reason, metaphysics here appears to be identified as having its roots in the reduction of manyness carried out by a people distinguished in history for the practice of monotheism.

The section *European Paideuma* thus reveals that Pound's anti-Semitism in the 1940s converges on the refutation of metaphysics. It also suggests that such anti-Semitism was nourished less by motives of Nazi-Fascist propaganda than by personal reflection. In his looking to European culture, Pound singles out a line of thought that is not always anti-Semitic but which he uses in an anti-Semitic manner. It is possible to single out a line using certain (Leibnizian) criticisms of Spinoza (letter to George Santayana), which Pound endows with anti-Semitic implications[47] and which takes account of the anti-Semitic polemic of Voltaire.[48] Pound's connection between language and monotheism as it appears in *Convenit esse Deos* is worth considering. Not yet recognized by scholars,[49] it compels us to reflect further on Pound's anti-Semitism. Here, Pound appears more notably to be drawing, and could very well be drawing, from an author who was already part of the Poundian encyclopedia — Ernest Renan[50] — who not only had identified monotheism as the culture of the Jews but had established a relationship between Jewish monotheism and the poverty of the Hebraic art binding language to religion, a bond which seems to be a point of reference for Poundian analysis. The volume to which I refer is *Histoire générale et système comparée des langues sémitiques*.[51] There is no evidence that Pound had read this text. Nevertheless, by posing relations among religion, art, and language, Renan's study formulated a type of analysis close to the one on which Pound was to concentrate, particularly by using Frobenius's concept of the organicity of culture (Paideuma). For Pound, it is in light of the organic concept of culture that the field of aesthetics assumes new importance. Through the identification of art as *technê*, the writings collected here exhibit the concreteness of Pound's effort to oppose and block the process of abstraction. It is an effort in which the field of art is entrusted with the task of healing a culture infected by the products of metaphysics. The critique of art as imitation, the critique of the concept of form, the denunciation of the depreciation of *technê* (which for Pound had played only a marginal role in Western culture) [52]—these are all stages of a process which by opposing art to metaphysics has as its goal the removal of what Pound sees as the problem of evil.

The Rejection of Metaphysics: A Pragmatic Aesthetics

At the end of the 1930s the published and unpublished letters of Pound indicate that the American philosopher George Santayana, who had left Harvard and had retired to live in Italy, had joined the company of Pound's friends and correspondents. An expatriate like Pound and reluctant to make new acquaintances, Santayana at first showed no particular enthusiasm for the impetuous Pound, nor for the poetry which, through D. Cory, Pound offered him.[53] But the Pound-Santayana correspondence of 1939 documents the beginning of a relationship that will continue into the St. Elizabeth's years and will be fundamental to the reconstruction of Pound's persistent and thorny polemic against metaphysics.[54] It seems to be for Santayana that Pound, during the first half of the 1940s, was preparing a little notebook in Italian, nine typed pages with handwritten notes, *Estetica Pragmatica di E.P.* (*Pragmatic Aesthetics of E.P.*), in which Pound recapitulated the fundamental stages of what he defined as his aesthetic system since 1910, locating the epicenter of such a system in the term FUNCTIONS.

Evidently, the text contains reasons, already confirmed elsewhere, for the distance that the poet put between his own research and that of his contemporaries. Those reasons had to do with abstraction as manifested in language, and terminology that has lost its meaning. The text proposed renewed attention to language as fundamental, even if, as far as the theoretical aspect was concerned, Pound preferred resorting to an indirect method, letting the texts he was putting forth speak for themselves and giving himself little space. Such a choice is evident in the care with which Pound had attended to the publication, printing, and republication of the work of E. Fenollosa. Through Fenollosa's essay on the Chinese ideogram, the poet was articulating an unfolding reflection on the language of poetry and on the tasks with which poetry came to be entrusted, in the "struggle against abstractions." In *Pragmatic Aesthetics*, Pound's postscript to the 1936 edition of *The Chinese Written Character* [55] was recalled and defined as "fundamental." The meaning of the adjective "pragmatic" was explained by rendering it as "function," meaning "what carries out a function," and for that reason being opposed to something merely theoretical. The text thus came to furnish a sort of organigram for the basis on which such an aesthetics was formulated. It was focused essentially on the importance of language and the relation between "truth" and "art" (p. 217).

Writing and Mathematics

Throughout that part of *Pragmatic Aesthetics* which came to be called *Part II* and was entitled *The Form of Thought or How to Think*, Pound, in reaffirming the importance of the "written language of China" (proposed by Fenollosa as an attack against abstraction), emphasizes the relation between writing and mathematics (arithmetic, algebra, and analytic geometry):

"mathematics   the writing
    arithmetic
    algebraic
    analytic"

In these relations, he notes the characteristics that writing should have and where the exact sciences must be substituted for the rules of rhetoric. The proposed relation connects writing and knowledge, where writing is associated not with the arts of the medieval trivium but with those related to the quadrivium, which Pound changes here by replacing astronomy and music with algebra and analytic geometry. The relation also substitutes the laws of the science of nature for those of rhetoric and grammar, with which medieval writing had been associated (the arts of the trivium being grammar, dialectic, and rhetoric). Under these new laws the qualitative relations pertaining to beautiful style are transformed into quantitative ones.

It must be understood that in *Vorticism* (1914), Pound had proposed that the word "vortex" was born of the necessity of giving a name to new types of relations, relations that went beyond, for example, the propositions of Euclidean geometry.[56] The approach of *Pragmatic Aesthetics* is of fundamental significance, not only where it brings an insight already present in the text on Vorticism to its coherent evolution but also and much more generally where it shows the new level of awareness the poet attained in the relation he had already proposed between literature and science, in the 1940s.

The disengaging of writing from grammar (already at work in Fenollosa) and Fenollosa's radical assertion that poetry is in accord with science rather than grammar was again confirmed. But here persistent points came into play. The first point has to do with a more precise insight into the concept of nature. This concept, drawn from and mirrored in physical science, takes into account the inquiry which from the nineteenth century applied analytical geometry to physics, thus signaling the end of the Hegelian and Romantic idea of nature and the beginning of the new scientific conception of nature.[57] The second point witnessed an evolution with respect to Fenollosa's text, where poetry, included in a wider discussion of written language, was put by Pound in relationship to the field of science in terms of mathematics.

Pound proceeded at first by developing the intuitions of Fenollosa, who regarded grammar as bound to logic,[58] and subsequently by proposing, in an agreement of poetry with science (through mathematics), the concrete realization of what had been put forth in the *ABC of Reading* (1934) as an embryonic project, that is, the comparison with the scientific method. If grammar was bound to logic and therefore to the syllogism, language as bound to grammar reveals—as we read in *Convenit esse Deos*—"the marks of the centuries of oppression" (p. 136). Fenollosa had written: "Poetry agrees with science and not with logic."

In the *ABC of Reading*, Pound had proposed the ideogrammic method as scientific inasmuch as it was a method of the detail and the particular. He had defined such a method as working through "comparison,"[59] but it is in *Pragmatic Aesthetics* that we find a more mature reflection and perhaps the ultimate theory. Here, by rescuing writing from the language of metaphysics, Pound ties it to the exact sciences, those sciences which ever since Galileo had guaranteed the knowledge of nature insofar as nature was written, according to Galileo,[60] "in mathematical language." For Pound, mathematics, algebra, and analytic geometry — having been put into relation with writing — become the rules that substituted the laws governing nature for the grammar derived from the syllogism. Careful inspection shows that it is the Baconian method that is developed implicitly along with a critique of this method. Bacon had replaced the deductive method proper to syllogism with the inductive method as the instrument for the knowledge of nature.[61] Pound brings language into a comparison with the new physical science, substituting the mathematical rules of nature for the rules of the science of metaphysics. Mathematical relations will preside over the written language.

In *Pragmatic Aesthetics*, Pound tries to resolve the shortcoming of the Renaissance: its failure to update language in light of the new science. In *How to Write*, the analytic geometry of Descartes, defined as "magnificent," is set in opposition to his language, defined as "poor." In "Ogden and Debabelization,"[62] the accusation is formulated as a betrayal. The "betrayal of the clerks"[63] lies in the comparison of language, which has been left to "sunbake and decompose" (p. 127). In *Pragmatic Aesthetics*, writing for the first time is defined in terms of exact science. From *Machine Art* to *Pragmatic Aesthetics*, the critique of abstract thinking is thus transformed into a project and plan for which the knowledge we gain through science is crucial.[64]

We will follow, from *Machine Art* onward, the development of Pound's project, focusing on the emergence of an aesthetics of *technê* in which the concepts of art and aesthetics itself come to be revised.

The Aesthetics of the Machine

Machine Art and Other Writings suggests a turning point in Pound's aesthetics. It takes form starting from the second half of the 1920s and begins by reconsidering the sphere of aesthetics as the sphere of practical and useful activity. This enlargement of the sphere of aesthetics focuses on two categories of Poundian reflection which are not to be found in the volumes of criticism or the already published prose writings. The first is the category of "function" (which originates with the essay *Machine Art*) as aesthetic value because it is a mechanism of producing a work ("energy"), and the second is the category of "plural," which we find in *Convenit esse Deos*. Both categories appear to be related to the analysis and refutation of metaphysics which is formulated in the various sections of the present book. They are developed through a fundamental reflection on form. Through such reflection, Pound confronts and substantiates the polemic against abstraction that began with Imagism.

Examination of the archive reveals that these categories, far from representing aspects of little importance to general Poundian reflection, form the basis of a reflection that unfolds continuously from the second half of the 1920s down to the 1940s and presides—I propose—over the *Rock-Drill* and *Thrones* sections of *The Cantos*. Placed in relation to *The Cantos* the two categories represent a crucial evolution of viewpoints formulated between 1914 and 1919. The category of mechanical function is connected with Vorticism, while the category of plural develops insights already proposed by Imagism and Fenollosa's reflections on language, which Pound had made his own by inserting Fenollosa's essay on *The Chinese Written Character* into his *Instigations* of 1920.[65]

Pound's concept of function appears in the essay *Machine Art*. From the second half of the 1920s, Pound proposes a conception of aesthetics in which beauty coincides with function: "We find a thing beautiful in proportion to its aptitude to a function" (p. 69). Form is important, not insofar as it is architectural, but insofar as it is able to carry out a function: "The 'machine' is in a much better state than is the accessory architecture of machinery . . . . Aptitude to a given end had forced or lured the inventor or inventors of line to a point nearer perfection" (p. 58). Attention is directed not to the architectural form of the machine, but to the "motor," which represents the point of latent and "concentrated energy" of the machine's function. The concept of "form" is bound to the critique of statics, but the emphasis is not so much on movement as it is on the mechanism, on which the form depends and which obeys a law determined not by the whim of the inventor but by the condition of producing a work: "The plastic of machines begins for a man the moment he stops to consider a machine as something looked at; and to ask himself whether its form is good to look at or annoying to look at, or to perceive *as form*" (p. 57).

The critique of the subjective in art which *Machine Art* puts forth, carrying to the extreme Imagism's imperative of depersonalization, is conducted by attaching one of the primary tenets of industrialism—to produce a work—to aesthetics.

Machine Art programmatically binds such a concept to the twentieth century. It is a fundamental text for the field of reflection which Pound proposes, and it is a further critique of Romanticism and of the subjective as the residue of a romantic conception of art, whose persistent disguises must be stripped away. The artist of the century will be an engineer and not an architect, assigning second place to the realization of architecture and first place to the realization of technology: "The best modern architects are, I suppose, almost universally the engineers . . . but the best engineers are possibly in our time the engineers of machinery . . . . But . . . our buildings are inferior to our machinery. And the architect's best lesson may very possibly lie in the machine" (pp. 71–72).

Art as *Technê*

Machine Art develops and resolves what the writings of the 1910s document: a fundamental attention to the significance and value of *form*. The historical sense postulated in *Vortex* (1914)[66] distinguishes this text from what can be read in these same years, as documented by the discussions in *The Little Review* (1927).[67] *Machine Art* establishes a new basis for the criterion of beauty. In light of the machine, Pound reactivates the division between art and beauty that had characterized the Greek and medieval worlds. He recovers for art the category of *technê*[68] and updates it for the modern machine. On the one hand, the machine confirms that art is "skill to make something" (*technê* as defined in Aristotle's *Nicomachaean Ethics* VI, iv); on the other, it imposes a new criterion of beauty, one that derives from a critique of the traditional concept of form. Pound takes up the celebrated proposition of functionalism: "we find a thing beautiful in proportion to its aptitude to a function" (p. 6). But at the same time, as Pound's library documents, he goes further in seeking the origin of functionalism in the philosophy of Bacon, who marks one of the crucial points in the opening up of the modern age. The critique of the concept of form is the key point on which Pound attacks one of metaphysics' strong points: beauty as the contemplation of an ideal realm, beauty as ideal form.[69] Pound transforms this concept of beauty into the notion of form as law. The beauty of the machine resides in its lawfulness and therefore in the production of "energy" (since the machine depends on the "motor," which always obeys the law for which the machine was made).

Machine Art proposes an aesthetics of *technê*, that is, an aesthetics in which art is the skill of making and beauty is aptness to purpose.[70] *Machine Art* must be read in light of the debate on the machine which took place in the United States during the 1920s, particularly in the pages of *The Little Review*, the literary magazine for which Pound was foreign editor from 1917 until 1920. The evolution in the perspective between the *Vorticism* of 1914 and *Machine Art* of the late 1920s should be seen in terms of the two different movements to which Pound looks, even as he simultaneously counteracts them: for Vorticism, Italian Futurism; for *Machine Art*, the German Bauhaus.[71]

In the 1920s, *The Little Review* was an organ by which European and German aesthetics were directly and indirectly transmitted to America. In 1924 the magazine published in two issues a long article—whose epigraph was dedicated "to Ezra Pound"—on the "Aesthetics of the Machine" by the French artist Fernand Léger.[72] Léger's article was mostly organized as a rethinking of some of the Bauhaus's programmatic assertions. It criticized the Renaissance's devaluation of mechanical arts and its imposition of a division between the fine and applied arts. Following one of the Bauhaus's crucial points, he emphasized the position of the craftsman, identifying the craftsman's work with the artist's.

Apparently, "Machine Art" does not take Léger's emphasis on craft into account. Aware of Morris and Ruskin on this topic, Pound attempts rather to update them. For Pound, the new craftsman is the engineer, and mostly he is trying to transfer into the motor the meaning of art as *technê*, that is, the kind of activity that is shared by craftsman and artist. If, according to Pound, the mechanical parts of the machine "and the foci of their action" show that they have been made by "thought over thought," the motor is the product of a long activity of research of intelligence. The motor, therefore, is the artificial intelligence that updates the work of the craftsman. At the same time, because the motor's concentrated intelligence is the result of research, observations, calculation, the machine relates the field of aesthetics to a type of knowledge proper to the scientific field, operational and also useful insofar as it functions. The photographs which Pound collected to illustrate the text explain his viewpoint to a greater extent because they are instruments of measurement (the pyrometer) or calculation, or single screws, particulars of mechanical parts. According to Pound, the motor's function relates art to the baggage of technical knowledge through which the functioning of the machine is made possible. In *Machine Art*, art encompasses a meaning that resembles the medieval concept of art, in which the word "art" was used to indicate an ensemble of knowledges (sciences) used by man, such as, for instance, the arts of the trivium (dialectic, rhetoric, grammar) or those of the quadrivium (music, astronomy, geometry, mathematics).

The concept of art as practical and useful activity is still present in the second section of *Machine Art*, where machines are related to music in terms of acoustic, that is, the technique of regulating and measuring sounds. The category of function explains Pound's relationship between the two sections. According to George Antheil, the American composer of *Ballet mécanique*, the form of music is time.[73] Pound focuses on the "great bass" as form because of the function it plays in transforming noise into sound.

Pound defines here the "great bass" as the frequencies below those that the ear has been accustomed to consider as notes.[74] Antheil's use of the "longer durations" is the "transition point," writes Pound, because their divisions of time "are so big that the NOISE (is) as it were swallowed up by them" (p. 79).

The notion of beauty emerging from *Machine Art* stems from the following: The engineers' "best form comes from the mathematic of strains" (p. 71). ("Strain is the deformation or change in shape of a material as a consequence of applied forces. . . . Strain is directly measurable" [*McGraw-Hill Encyclopedia of Science and Technology* ⟨New York: 1992⟩].) In this assertion lies a turning point in Pound's concept of aesthetics at the end of the 1920s. It is less a question of putting the meaning of form in connection with mechanical tensions ("strains") than of looking at these tensions in terms of mathematics. Mathematics is seen here not as mathematical harmony already variously recalled, but as mathematics of strains, of misusable tensions. *Vortex* had introduced mechanism and efficiency. In *Vorticism*, the relationship with the field of mathematics was largely comparative, while in *Machine Art*, mathematics changes the perspective in resolving the concept of form in relations of measurement of applied tensions (strains). The brief statement I have cited will preside over the more important perspective upon which *Pragmatic Aesthetics* focuses. There, the laws of mathematics and its functions will preside over writing.

Art as Production

In the second and third sections of *Machine Art*, machines are suggested as means of "production." Their meaning vis-à-vis economic values of overproduction shows the influence of the economic ideas of A. Orage and C. H. Douglas. Such ideas connecting art and economy, already active in British culture mostly through Ruskin and Morris, appear to be reconsidered through Douglas's theories: the positive result of industry is production, which, in Pound's assumption, opposes usury.[75] In *The ABC of Economics*, Pound affirms "overproduction did not begin with the industrial system, nature habitually overproduces."[76] In *Machine Art*, medieval organization is recalled as an organization of production and compared with that of the Ford Motor Company: "An organization like Henry Ford's is probably feudal. I use the word here with a sense of relatively very high commendation; it implies the responsibility of the overlord to his vassals, and implies a very different mode of thought from that implied in the abusive term 'industrial system' of industrialism" (p. 80).

The machine as productive of work is therefore also productive of leisure: "Machines were made to eliminate work and produce leisure." The artificial, which comes to improve nature, is the means by which Pound's modernism tries to resolve the cause of evil in history: usury and avarice.[77] That Pound in his correspondence[78] considered *Machine Art* as a writing on American art shows his continuing faith in the United States as the land of a New Renaissance and a new economy (a notion outlined in *Patria Mia* [1913]).[79] The broadening of aesthetics is considered in an economic light; as Pound notes, "The social implement of a machine age is perception of economics."[80]

Modern art appears to tie technology to *technê* by way of an updating of the Greek concept of art. Because the focus of machines is located in the motor, this word introduces the concept of "energy" shared by both machine and nature. In Aristotle, nature contains in itself the generative principle, while the art object does not.[81] *Machine Art* takes up this distinction, because the motor as the focus of energy is akin to the productive power of nature. In *Rock-Drill, Canto 85*, this relationship is still at work. Nature as the process of growth is connected to *technê*,[82] thus supporting a kind of osmosis between the generative process of nature and man's productive activity. From *Machine Art* onward, aesthetics comes to embody a field of relations which in themselves oppose usury—usury being in opposition of production, according to Pound's definition in *Canto 45*.[83]

From *Machine Art* onward, the field of aesthetics is organized as an inclusive whole. While it encompasses the concept of art as making, as science, and as production, it sets up at the same time a series of oppositions. As practical activity of intelligence, art is opposed to a theoretical knowing; as purposeful and rule-bound, it is opposed to subjectivity; as production, it is opposed to usury. This aesthetics is therefore pragmatic at first, because it reveals its essence in an acting which is also a counteracting. Pound's use of the term "function" in his aesthetics suggests that this function implies a working against the field to be opposed, that is, the field Pound indicates as that of abstraction.

How to Write

In *How to Write*, Pound evaluates the cognitive function of the language of poetry. In this writing, Imagism is proposed as a contribution by Pound and his generation to 'realism,' a contribution designated as a "struggle against 'abstraction'" (p. 103). In this writing and in other fragments collected in the same section under the title *Addenda*, Pound proposes that the new cognitive level deriving from the sciences has to be extended to the language used by the literati: "The next movement in literature . . . the problem upon which the best writers are already engaged is that of carrying into literature the advantages of science" (p. 110). The laboratory of the scientist is the focus of the new knowledge which must take form in language: "Today . . . the biologist can think many things, can know many things which he finds it quite impossible to convey by language" (p. 110). It is in the laboratory of the scientist that Fenollosa's concept of nature is updated and the relation between poetry and science is substantiated. This concept of nature includes the knowledge of nature that comes from the laboratory of the chemist and the biologist.

Pound's evolution regarding Fenollosa's position on the language of poetry[84] is enlarged to embrace an attention to the historical problem of written language. *How to Write* puts forth the fundamental assertion that language must be related to the level of knowledge; that is, to a new level of knowledge there must correspond a language that conveys that level and does not obfuscate it. Such a correspondence is related to the ancient dispute between realism and nominalism. Various strata and levels of knowledge are identified so that they may take form in language.

Following Fenollosa's precedent, Pound asserts the necessity of naming the *"thing"* not in the "abstract" but by articulating its various components. At the same time, he precisely defines the necessity of leaving intact the intrinsic unity of the thing. For Pound, the convincing example seems to be that of the Leibnizian monad,[85] which furnishes an example of something at once one and many (plural): "a real thought (Leibnizian monad of thought every active incapable of being compressed out of existence etc.) as distinct from a mere cliche or imperfect verbal manifestation consists of a pattern or *group* of related images . . ." (p. 103).

The plural that emerges here in connection with language is a category which through various formulations is present in the other sections of the book, plural being the foundation for what we have indicated as Pound's analysis and rejection of metaphysics.

Poetry and *Techné*

Machine Art suggests that *techné*, the idea of art as construction, is at the center of reflection in Pound's synchronous formulation of the famous categories of *poieō* ("melopoeia, phanopoeia, logopoeia") as the structure of his poetics. After writing *How to Read* and before *ABC of Reading*, Pound reformulated these categories in *How to Write*, which contains a further, stronger reflection on language.

How to Write seems to be a treatise on poetics reformulated in light of *techné*. According to what Pound wrote in *Pragmatic Aesthetics*, *How to Read* was Pound's attempt to reject the Aristotelian categories of poetics. That is, as one draft of *How to Read* shows, melopoiea, logopoiea, phanopoiea are opposed to imitation.[86] By taking up the Greek word *poieō* [87] (which means to do, and also to make, to produce), Pound brings poetry face to face with the old meaning of the Greek word *poiesis* before its crystallization into genre.[88] In Greek culture, *poieō* and *technê* both include the meaning of an activity of generating, producing, and of making something. Aristotle utilizes two different words to distinguish the production of art from the production of nature; however, both words have the meaning of producing something. The word "poiesis" is utilized for the generation of nature; "technê" is utilized for the production of art.

If *technê* opposes *mimesis*, poetry, like art, is considered a making instead of an imitative activity. But a relationship with nature is still alive insofar as poetry appears in Pound to be considered as included in nature's generative-productive process.[89] Therefore, if poetry and art are human constructions, then insofar as the rules of this construction are human rules, they must reflect those presiding over nature. If to engage in "logopoiea" is "to charge language with meaning," then language will be saturated with nature (as we know it through scientific knowledge); it will be carried back to that unity of word and thing which, according to Pound, Aristotelian metaphysics obstructs. The Chinese have demonstrated in their language the excellence of "phanopoiea," but the West must adopt a different course: it must realize a "logopoiea" that absorbs the quality of the Chinese ideogram in a nonideogrammic language. The important section of *How to Write* is the second, which offers concrete proposals for realizing such a course. The text outlines "intuitive judgement" not as something final but, in its interaction with reason, it reveals that discourse on "How to Write" enters into a vaster discourse on knowledge. Here, intuitive knowledge, far from being proposed as the form of knowledge proper to the aesthetic sphere, is regarded as the manifold which operates in cerebral activity. A relation is posited between knowledge and gestalt, that is, the form of thought is conceived as an organic plurality. The monad of Leibniz is recalled as a plural unity that gathers the manifold of the existent. But—and this point must be thoroughly appreciated—this knowledge for Pound does not contrast with scientific knowledge. Just as *technê* is not opposed to nature inasmuch as nature is an activity of producing, a homology is also suggested between an intuitive and at the same time rational knowledge which feeds on the manifold, on the plurality provided by sense data, and the nature of matter which reveals its pluri-relational being. In this, a further contribution to a literal definition of logopoiea—"to make the word"—is *How to Write*'s proposal to charge language with the new knowledge derived from scientific knowledge.

The center of the new knowledge that must enter into language lies in the knowledge of matter, which derives from the laboratory of the scientist. "Logopoiea" will mean making the word according to the laws of relation revealed by nature; it will not *imitate* nature, but it will instead draw on the laws presiding over nature. The scientist's laboratory uncovers the laws which preside in the configurations of matter. The nature of matter is revealed in scientific knowledge, and the knowledge of nature and of nature's laws is in and from science.

Writing and Science: Art as Biology

Pound seeks here to establish a relation between literature and science, one formulated as method and as content and emphasized in the entire section *How to Write*. It is especially evident in the *Addenda* through notes which Pound wrote in thinking about integrating and making connections between the various parts of his critical work for an edition of his complete prose works.[90] Because the project failed to be realized, Pound wrote *How to Write* to take up the main points of his criticism. The text, whose appendix was to have contained the republication of Fenollosa's text, seems to be proposed as a second section of a projected book, of which *How to Read* would have been the first.

For this reason, the section *How to Write* is in large part a mosaic tile fitting between *How to Read* and *ABC of Reading*. The latter, written in 1934, was intended by Pound to surpass *How to Read*. There, the enunciation of "the ideogrammic or scientific method" comes to condense the marginal notes collected here. Although repudiated by Pound, these notes are in reality bearers of a message which the *ABC of Reading*'s ideogrammic method develops but whose sense and course are partially lost, at least as far as the most important aspect of these fragments is concerned.

Many assertions here seem to be more dashed off than thought out (as, for instance, "art is part of biology" [p. 67]); nevertheless, an essentially composite inlay emerges from these diverse fragments. In one part, we read the suggestion that the activity of thinking is gestalt, that is, form as the organicity of diverse entities. This thinking is not the abstract thinking of syllogistic logic but instead stresses biological logic. Such biological logic, suggested in the postscript to Rémy de Gourmont[91] as the sphere of sensibility which operates in intelligence, is opposed both to traditional logic and to that logic returned to by such contemporary thinkers as Bertrand Russell.[92] But it is in modern science that Pound finds further proof for the condemnation of syllogistic logic. The accomplishment of this science of matter lies in revealing relations and plural associations (*Addenda*). The relation between the dynamics and potentialities of matter, and the correspondence which Pound establishes with mental activity in the same fragment (p. 120), comes to locate in the science of matter the repudiation of the syllogistic logic on which Western language is built. As a substitute for such logic, Pound puts forth what he calls in another fragment "relation biological" (*Addenda*, p. 112). To the abstract logic of the syllogism is opposed a new biological logic, where biology speaks of living organicity and plurality. In *How to Write*, the "failure of literature" as opposed to the success of scientific knowledge is the subject of a further discourse on language.

The entire *How to Write* propounds a relation between literature and science in which language must be made to conform to modern scientific knowledge. This knowledge includes the already recalled science of matter consigned to the laboratory of the scientist and the new science of nature, physics, which compels time to enter into the gestalt of space. The recalled theory of relativity signals oblique cuts of knowledge which nevertheless are of value in enlarging the field of knowledge. Poetry and art are biology in that they are related to the living and are productions and constructions of human biology. *How to Write* establishes the path Pound followed toward cementing the relation between logic and language and proposing a new logic based on modern science. The rejection of metaphysics at one level takes its place in this position against logic—which Pound had already faced indirectly when he translated and wrote a postscript to Rémy de Gourmont in 1921—and in the 1930s Pound enriched and made this position more complex. *How to Write* recalls the postscript to Rémy de Gourmont and connects it to Fenollosa. The two names are complementary and reveal both foci of the polemic against the logic of syllogism and its language. In *How to Write*, a section devoted to "phanopoeia" is much longer than that in *How to Read*, and more complete than that devoted to "melopoiea." The word "logopoiea" is not used in *How to Write*, but the whole third section appears to be a further reflection on that concept already defined in *How to Read* as the intellect's dance among words.[93] This third section returns to the relation between knowledge and language and the importance of the knowledge that comes from science to the search for a new logic.

The New Logic: A Biological Logic

It must be emphasized that a firmly held point of Pound's discourse is that he does not oppose an intuitive but a "biological" logic to the logic of the syllogism. It is possible to reconstruct what Pound meant by biological as opposed to syllogistic relations through several fragments (*Addenda*) assembled here in the section entitled *How to Write*. They must be connected to the postscript to Rémy de Gourmont, which is an essential step toward Pound's idea of biological logic. In the postscript, Pound sums up his viewpoint in a note: "The skull does not hold all the human intelligence,"[94] thus implying that the sphere of sensibility must be counted as a form of intelligence.[95] The postscript investigates this sensibility through visionary activity, which realizes itself in a mystical activity productive of visions.[96] Such visions were regarded as one form of cognitive activity. On the basis of these reflections, in which knowledge and creation were identified with the production of an image,[97] Pound some years later formulated one of the categories of *poieō*—phanopoiea.[98] Distinct from and complementary to logopoiea, it delimited the other creative level that, together with melopoiea, structured Pound's poetics. The postscript formulated, then, the intuitive level of sensibility as a contribution to the making of intelligence. Love as the center of the emotions provided the sensuous basis for intelligence, which basis was reorganized afterward by cerebral activity. The instinct studied by Gourmont as a form of crystallized intelligence ("in Gourmont's exposition the instinct is not something opposed to intellect," p. 51), provides one of the many sources of data that the nervous system collects and the brain reorganizes.[99] But at the end of the 1920s, on the basis of the science of matter studied in those years (connecting biology with chemistry and physics), Pound ultimately comes to connect biology with a biological logic as a relating of many connections revealed in the scientific laboratory. The plural relations in Gourmont, suggested as plural data furnished by sensibility, are now proposed as relations constitutive of the nature of matter.

Biological logic, insofar as it is proper to the living, presides over both knowledge and written language. The knowledge of the structure of matter centers on the cells studied by the scientist in his laboratory. These cells are put forth as correlated and updating primitive man's idea of nature. By appropriating the biology of the cell, Pound's biological logic discloses a homology between mind and matter. As a production of the mind, language comes to be compared to this new science of matter: "That is to say L-Bruhl, the savage with his wood and river; where the biologist is in New York in 1930 with his cells (is at first sight) in relation to language. Or in relation to cells regarding, in reference language" (p. 106). If poetry is language carried to the maximum of meaning, then this meaning derives also from an updating of language in light of the new science of matter.

The repudiation of the syllogism in light of the science of matter is seen as bound to the condemnation of abstractions, which tend to reduce the many to the one. According to one of Fenollosa's critiques, which Pound emphasized, Aristotle's logic is in the service of metaphysics.[100] In his copy of the *Novum Organum*, Pound underscores in various ways the ties between logic and metaphysics. *How to Write* was presented as bringing about a revolution equal in importance to that of Bacon; it sought to update language on the basis of the new science: "However platitudinous my present formulation the thing I am driving at is not platitude. Properly understood, it can be as important for the individual having patience enough to hunt for a meaning, as important for the actual thinking to come as was Bacon's formulation for the extension of scientific knowledge" (p. 104).

As the basis of knowledge, *How to Write* places organicity and plurality, rationality, and the imponderabilia: "One's final judgment is 'intuitive'? Or shall I say one's final judgment is made up of a certain number of formulatable reasons and a certain penumbra of imponderabilia" (p. 102). The form of thinking as a "Gestalt" of a plurality includes reason and intuition. Through this term, Pound refers to the Gestalt psychology that became influential in 1920s Germany; although he kept his distance from the movement, asserting that probably among Gestaltists the group image was not put in relation to thought (p. 103).[101] Starting from *How to Write*, the activity of thinking, seen in light of the science of matter, imposes a new reflection on written language. The more recent biological research is the disquieting center of reflection which seems not to be dominated by the same poet. In *The ABC of Reading* this center is so compressed and condensed as to be virtually incomprehensible to the reader.[102] It is nevertheless operative as a reference point for Pound's writing of the *Cantos*. The heart of Pound's biological logic goes well beyond the anthropological viewpoint still present in Rémy de Gourmont. For Pound, the plurality of relations found in the biology of cells furnishes biological proof of the untruth of the syllogism, because the syllogism fails to correspond with nature as revealed by biology: "Il y a plusieurs plans. Relation biological, not syllogistic . . . . Syllogistic relation does not exist between natural phenomena" (p. 112).

The new science of nature to which Pound looks seems to be a combination of biology and physics. The new researches, which in those years connected psychology with biology and physics,[103] had to be considered as one of the sources of these scattered fragments. *How to Write* asks us to consider that Pound's "ideogrammic or scientific method" includes reflections active in this unfinished text. The "ideogrammic" method put forth in *The ABC of Reading* appears to be used to formulate, on the basis of the ideogram (which Fenollosa indicated as one and plural), that organic plurality which Pound sees presiding over biology as well as logic, thanks to the correspondence between thought and biology, the activity of mind confronted with the atoms and the potential of matter: "Nature of mind to move, of matter to stop; of mind to be incapable of conceiving a limit whereat stop is possible . . . but in consideration of matter the moment mind gets 'into it,' i.e., into the consideration begins to discover potentials and dynamisms, as p.e. in atom" (p. 120).

"Emphasis Is on the Plural"

From *How to Write* on, one can trace the significance which the category of plural came to assume for Pound in the 1930s. It is inserted in the more general context of the rejection of abstractions, and at the same time it develops one of the crucial points by means of which Pound's polemic against abstractions constructs a structural polemic against metaphysics. Such a category may be assumed to be a center of the reflection which runs through the sections. *How to Write* proposed that this category of plural must be established in language. In *Convenit esse Deos*, Pound states a more radical relation, where plural is opposed to the monotheistic creed. Programmatically, the writing starts with the following assertion: "My emphasis is on the plural" (p. 135). Once this category has been identified, we may go back to Pound's analysis on written language as it emerges from these scattered fragments and verify that Pound's polemic against the language of abstraction as well as his anti-Semitic polemic are built on the same crucial point—the rejection of the method and content of metaphysics as responsible for the abstract thought and language of the West.

Language and Anti-Semitism

In 1934's *Ogden and Debabelization*, Pound offers a concise diagnosis: the new Babel consists in the gap between what is known and what enters into language. "The betrayal of the clerks" for Pound lies in the confrontation with language. Scattered observations organize a coherent thought focusing on two points: (1) the relation between modernity and language, a relation hitherto disregarded; and (2) the relation between nature and language. Modernity and nature come to be identified in the sense that "modern" coincides with the relation to nature opened by the culture of the Renaissance and its science of nature. Pound locates in Christianity the first caesura on the journey to modernity. The word "verbum" is seen as an action which takes things out of eternity and locates "them somewhere in time" (p. 127). Carried over into language, this means that the cognitive and linguistic epicenter of the Christian era is to be found in the verb rather than the noun.

The second caesura is located in the post-Baconian era and is critical of the Renaissance for not treating the thing-terminology, which, according to Pound, had been alive in the Middle Ages. The new science of nature would place the renovation of language at the very base of the new science.

In *How to Write* the critique of the syllogism is thus bound to the critique of the cognitive process of Aristotelian logic insofar as this logic is constructed on the deductive chain of reasoning (abstraction) which sacrifices the multiplicity of that which is known directly for a general unknown. In proposing the "verb" as the epicenter of the modern era (*Ogden and Debabelization*), Pound makes an implicit critique (echoing Fenollosa's) of another point of the Aristotelian Organum, *De Interpretatione*, where the noun was seen as the essence of nature and the verb itself was considered as noun.[104] Substituting verb for noun, plural (unity) for the One, biologic logic for the syllogistic, Pound banishes from language the predicates of Aristotelian substance of metaphysics, which is one and immobile.

Through *Convenit esse Deos* we are asked to consider the homology between Pound's analysis of language and knowing and his analysis of Western culture. Pound's analysis of written language and the solutions which he proposed, along with his analysis of culture, show a precise correspondence. Pound's anti-Semitism, at least in its post-1930s' formulation, appears to be based primarily on the rejection of the same categories he banished from language and is closely tied to the polemic against Aristotelian metaphysics and Aristotle's monotheism, the responsibility for which in Western history Pound attributed to Jewish monotheism.

In *Convenit esse Deos*, Pound stresses the comparison between language, thought, and religion, finding in this comparison the confirmation of the organicity proposed by Frobenius. In language, thought, and religion, he finds the signs of the betrayal of nature to the extent that monotheism is also a betrayal of nature. The language of the West, insofar as it is the product of monotheistic and dogmatic thinking, is the language of metaphysics. To Pound's analysis corresponds the attempt at a solution with two points of operation—belief and language.

In the section *European Paideuma*, Pound proposes the following theses:

(A)   The rejection of monotheism.
(B)   Abstract thinking imposes the idea of oneness and the reduction of plurality to the One.
(C)   The relation between the metaphysics of Aristotle and the monotheism of the Jews, the Jews being seen as responsible for the monotheistic thought of the West.
(D)   The relations between monotheism, logic, and language.
(E)   The existence in Christianity of a non-monotheistic tradition stifled by Jewish monotheism.
(F)   The existence in Europe of a religion of nature that admits a plurality of gods and, in turn, the need to recover such a tradition.

Pound's Novum Organum

The analyses are functionally linked. The translations of Confucius are an attempt to inject a tradition of a natural religion into the West. This attempt is carried out in the section *European Paideuma*. "I am for a Confucian treatment of Christianity," writes Pound. The radio talks in the same years tend to isolate the nucleus of the error and its consequences. The "Confucian organum" becomes the tool.

European Paideuma responds to this intention. A technique which we may define as semiotic permits him to find a natural religion in the rites of rebirth and regeneration still alive in the popular cultural practices of Rapallo. Here, Pound sees a continuity between a natural religion present in the Greek world and a natural religion in the here-and-now. But it is not only a matter of evaluating the centrality of natural religion insofar as living practices speak of rites of rebirth through the preservation of the seed. It is also a matter of seeing that the productive forces of nature are implicitly opposed to usury. *European Paideuma* demonstrated for Pound the vitality of the old continent, contrary to Spengler's thesis of a decline ("To Hell with Spengler").[105] On this basis, the possibility of interacting with the Confucian model not only comes to have meaning but can be assured of success. The sense of the writings of these years and of Pound's contemporaneous effort to publish the works of Confucius is revealed in a phrase dashed off in a letter to Santayana: "[to place the new] in taking a known axis of reference."[106] In this way the intention is to create an awareness of this still living tradition in order to insert the new. This, indicated by Pound as the *Confucianum Organum*, adumbrates Pound's *Novum Organum*.

Pound centers at first on the tradition of natural religion in Europe and more importantly on the fact that such religion is based on and gives rise to pluralistic rather than monistic thinking. This is the same pluralism contained in Catholic culture. Catholicism, writes Pound, is Trinitarian and thus derives from a negative relation to its Semitic ancestry (*[Catholicism]*). Against monotheism, Pound counterposes the idea of the plural. If the Chinese language is the product of a culture based on a natural religion, *Confucianum Organum* reveals its meaning in light of the *European Paideuma* and presupposes the long reflection on the language of the ideogram as plural and relational.

Confucian China is used to indicate the course to follow for Pound's antidote to metaphysics. The entire method is alive in the ideogram, a language that is the product of a cultural tradition alien to any metaphysical implication. The Chinese ideogram points out the direction insofar as it is the product of the culture of "Chung Young."[107] This—according to Pound—is a culture that places nature and man at the center of philosophy and sees in nature a law, an "unvarying," "unwobbling norm" ("that's what Chung Young means") which is the "basis for science and foresight." Pound's focusing in this radio speech on the uniform process of nature establishes in the "norm" of nature the law which will preside not just over nature but over ethics and language. But it is the word "science" Pound introduces which shows us that Confucius' method contains Pound's method. *Confucianum Organum* pronounces through the Chinese philosopher the Poundian organum as put into focus in the 1940s. The Poundian organum will work through this unifying law of nature as researched by modern physics and biology. It will construct the language that this new type of knowledge requires and imposes. The laws of physics and mathematics will preside over it.

"Truth": Science and "Art" as "Truth"

The new *organum* is already operating in *Pragmatic Aesthetics*, in which the connection between science and language returns, focusing on the relation between "truth" and "art." The term "truth" further clarifies the significance of the relation of science to language. If the art-truth relation is indispensable, how can we attain truth, and what is Pound's notion of truth? For Pound, truth does not exist outside what is known by man. The problem, above all, is to be taken up by language, since language is entrusted with the articulation and transmission of truth. In Dante's letter to Can Grande della Scala, which Pound recalls in *Pragmatic Aesthetics* à propos of the truth-art relation, Dante defined truth as "*quia veritas de re . . . est similitudine perfeta rei sicut est.*"[108] That is, truth is the agreement between things and words. Pound often recalls the medieval statement "*nomina sunt consequentia rerum,*" which he attributes to Thomas Aquinas.

According to Pound, scientific knowledge makes it possible for us to attain this truth. Pound here follows what Popper calls "the Galilean method," according to which science holds the rank of knowing reality[109]—a view also found in Einstein.[110] Pound ascribes to writing the same rules that prevail in the sciences, rules that make scientific knowledge possible. Written language is put into a relation with the exact sciences, because the aim of language is, like science, to reach truth.

In *Pragmatic Aesthetics*, writing and aesthetics are worked out in terms of operations. Writing finds its rules in mathematics, whose traditional field is that of measuring quantity. Arithmetic is the calculation of numerical values, while algebra deals with functions. Analytic geometry applies algebra as the study of functions to problems of measurement. (For the meaning of these terms as they were used in Pound's day, I am using the *Encyclopaedia Britannica* edition of 1912 as a source of popular knowledge in the 1930s.) *Pragmatic Aesthetics* advances in the direction opened up by *Machine Art*. If the beautiful is no longer that to which we look in contemplation, then aesthetics is pragmatic in that it focuses on relations that measure in terms of quantity and operations.

The term "pragmatic" which Pound uses to define his aesthetics also reveals, then, a boundary that delimits it. This theme returns in the correspondence with Santayana: "at the focus of the 'poEm' he [Pound] wants to put, not 'the KNOWABLE,' but that which 'I KNOW.'"[111] *Pragmatic Aesthetics* suggests that Pound—in being opposed to the thinking of Croce, "Point of view very different from Croce's point of view" (p. 155), to the Crocean hierarchy, which, as stated in the text, assigns the higher point of knowledge to philosophy instead of art[112]—seems to take up certain points of another Italian philosopher, Giambattista Vico, as mediated through Gentile's reading in *Studi vichiani*. But *Pragmatic Aesthetics* is not understandable without referring it to Pound's late 1930s reading of Aristotle's *Nicomachaean Ethics* and his subsequent focusing on *technê*.[113]

Pound's *Pragmatic Aesthetics*: Some Hypotheses Toward Its Reconstruction

Pragmatic Aesthetics is an unfinished text. However, we know from what Pound wrote in it and from marginal notes on the manuscript that Pound intended to define the whole of his aesthetic inquiry by means of the adjective "pragmatic." Pound's recalling in the text of the correspondence with George Santayana is crucial in our attempt to reconstruct this unfinished text. Because the definition of aesthetics as pragmatic belongs only to the early 1940s, a connection could be established between this definition and Pound's synchronous insistence in identifying in the exclusion of *technê* from Aristotle's *Magna Moralia* the starting point of the West's decadence.[114] If, according to Pound's reading of the *Nicomachaean Ethics, technê* is the kind of intelligence that realizes itself in doing and making, aesthetics is pragmatic because of its being related to a concept of art focused on from *Machine Art* onward, that is, an intelligence of making which is in itself a knowing. Pound's making connections in a letter to Santayana between "*technê*" and "grouped things" as expressions of a more secure knowledge opposing for that Western decadence confirms that *technê* is related to the problem of knowledge.[115] A revision of the concept of aesthetics is therefore suggested on these connections.

Pragmatic Aesthetics attempts to summarize Pound's opposition to the West's tendency to value the theoretical as the highest form of knowledge, counterposing to that the knowledge of art. If, as Pound writes, "art achieves a MORE PRECISE manifestation" than philosophy ("philosophy . . . [is] nothing but a vague fluid approximation," p. 159), we see that a revision of the concept of aesthetics comes from the revision of the concept of art. Art, in fact, becomes the highest form of knowledge. But whereas for Aristotle the highest form of knowledge was not practical but theoretical,[116] Pound regards the highest knowledge as "artistic" (in the sense of practical-productive intelligence), which encompasses the other levels of knowing. Constructing and knowing are identified—one knows in the very moment that one makes. If *technê* presides over the concept of art, if what emerges from these writings is an aesthetics of *technê,* then the field of aesthetics is not delimited by the beautiful. *Technê* is tied to Vico's notion that identifies intellection and work ("*intelligentia et opus*"). In opposition to Croce, Pound not only rejects the view that art is an intuitive moment preceding the moment of philosophic knowing (as Croce proposed), but he posits art as the highest knowing because it includes every human's form of knowing (both rational and intuitive) which realizes itself in making.

Through the texts collected here, the primacy of aesthetics turns out to be a synthesis of Poundian reflection that binds aesthetics to ethics and connects art with history.[117] The fact that *technê* had been scorned in Western thought ever since Aristotle's *Magna Moralia*[118] is for Pound one of the manifestations of metaphysics and avarice. If history and man as *polymetis* are expressions of art and *technê,* that is, of an intelligence that realizes itself in the act of knowing, which is in itself an act of making and producing, then avarice and usury, insofar as these are opposed to all productivity ("usury not having any regard to production," Canto 45), are also opposed to the very fruitfulness of human nature. In this way, Pound not only opposes good and evil in terms of opposition between nature and usury, but he opposes the fruitfulness of human history, man's self-realization in its various forms, to the avarice that impedes this history. *Pragmatic Aesthetics* embodies the idea of the Poundian sense of epic in the 1940s. The epic—for Pound a poem that includes history in the 1930s—structures in the 1940s the sense of history on waging war on the persisting metaphysics of the West.

Notes

1 The dates in parentheses are partially indicated by Pound and partially suggested by my research. I return to this dating in Notes to Texts. *Pragmatic Aesthetics of E.P.* is henceforth indicated as *Pragmatic Aesthetics.*

2 *The New Review* 1 (Winter 1931–1932): 292–293, an issue dedicated to machines, to which Pound contributed a brief note and fifteen photographs. Pound's note reprt. in Harriet Zinnes, ed., *Ezra Pound and the Visual Arts* (New York: New Directions, 1980).

3 See Donald Gallup, *A Bibliography* (Charlottesville: University Press of Virginia, 1983), 449–450.

4 Maria Luisa Ardizzone's *Ezra Pound e la scienza* (Milan: Scheiwiller, 1987), 104–151, contains the text dated 1927 by Pound. The text here is the revised version done by Pound in 1930.

5 Leonard Doob, ed., *Ezra Pound Speaking: Radio Speeches of World War II* (Westport, Conn.: Greenwood Press, 1978).

6 At the end of the 1920s, Pound planned a twelve-volume collection of his critical writings. In 1929 the first volume appeared, containing a reprint of one section of *The Spirit of Romance,* and *How to Read.* After that, the project was halted, apparently owing to a disagreement with the publisher. See Gallup, *A Bibliography,* 452. Pound's organizational plan for the volumes is documented in BRBL. "*The Prose Writings of E.P.* Gathered, Revised, as some might say Corrected or at least Castigated; with a Commentary by the Author and an Apology for his former timidities." Folders: "Collected Prose," 2934–2946.

7 Ezra Pound, *The ABC of Reading* (New Haven, Conn.: Yale University Press, 1934).

8 "An Image is that which presents an intellectual and emotional 'complex' in an instant of time" (1913; reprt. *Literary Essays* [New York: New Directions, 1954], 4). Pound said here that he took the term "complex" from the English psychologist Bernard Hart.

9   Giambattista Vico, *Principi di scienza nuova* (1744), chap. 10, in *Opere*, ed. Fausto Nicolini (Milan and Naples: Ricciardi, 1953), 439: "La filosofia contempla la ragione, onde viene la scienza del vero; la filologia osserva l'autoritá dell'umano arbitro, onde viene la coscienza del certo" ("Philosophy utilizes reason, from which we have the science of truth; philology is observant of the authority of human will, and from that we hold the science of the certain"; my translation).

10 The volumes of Pound's personal library are preserved in PB and in HRHR.

11 In "A Few Don'ts" (1913) (*Literary Essays,* 5) Pound advises poets to go "in fear of abstractions," and in *How to Write* he proposes his work and that of his generation as a "struggle against abstraction."

12 *Vortex* (1914); *Vorticism* (1914). *Vorticism* was inserted by Pound in *Gaudier-Brzeska: A Memoir* (London: John Lane, 1916), 81–94. "Vortex" is reprt. in Zinnes, ed., *Ezra Pound and the Visual Arts*, 151–152.

13 Fenollosa's essay was first published by Pound in four issues of *The Little Review* (1919). The following year Pound inserted the essay as an appendix to his *Instigations of Ezra Pound together with an Essay on the Chinese Written Character by Ernest Fenollosa* (New York: Boni and Liveright, 1920), 357–388. The 1936 edition, which included Pound's foreword and notes, has been published as the first volume in the proposed "Ideogrammatic Series, edited by Ezra Pound" for the English publisher Stanley Nott. See Gallup, *A Bibliography,* 159.

14 In *Addenda*, we read: "grubby-handed professors ... ignorant of art ... ignorant of language and of music, they drag in *metaphysics*, though they would not and possibly could not discuss *metaphysics* or physics with anyone trained in philosophical dialect of exact science of observation" (emphasis mine).

15 According to the evidence of his library, Pound read Aristotle's *Metaphysics* in different editions and at different periods. The following Italian edition is preserved at PB: Aristotle, *Introduzione alla filosofia*, ed. Armando Carlini (Bari: Laterza, 1925). This book contains selected chapters of the *Metaphysics* with several reading marks and notes by Pound. Other volumes (in HRHR) are *La metafisica*, ed. Armando Carlini (Bari: Laterza, 1928), which contains several reading marks and glosses by Pound. From the affixed stamp that shows the price of postage, dated 1940, it can be construed that Pound purchased the Carlini edition in the forties. Aristotle, *The Metaphysics, Books X–XIV,* trans. H. Tredennick. *The Oeconomica* and *Magna Moralia,* trans. G. Cyril Armstrong. (Cambridge, Mass.: Harvard University Press, 1935); original Greek on the facing page, marks by Pound on the Greek and on the English sides.

Pound's reading of Carlini's edition of Aristotle's *Metaphysics* in the 1940s is of particular relevance because of the line of thought which it suggests. Pound's reading marks show that he is following three main directions. (1) The development of Aristotle's theory of substance of metaphysics, one and immobile and eternal. (2) Features of Aristotle's thought which Pound sees as connected to Cavalcanti's *Donna mi prega.* The perceived connection to Cavalcanti is mostly evident in Pound's reading of the *Metaphysics,* Book VII, which contains Aristotle's theory of the accident (accident being the definition of love as given by Cavalcanti in *Donna mi prega*"). The third direction is implicit in Pound's annotations to Aristotle's concept of production, the Greek word being *poiesis*, which Carlini introduces in a note to Book VII, chap. 7, 225, to clarify the many relationships which Aristotle is bringing into focus through this word. Some quotations from the *Metaphysics* allow us to follow Pound's annotations to Aristotle's development of the idea of substance. After this, I will follow another aspect of Aristotelian thought, which we may indicate as *poiesis* and generation. Pound considered the two nuclei as opposites; the concept of substance, one and immobile, is individuated as being the opposite of Aristotle's theory of nature as generation and art as production. The former excludes movement and the temporal dimension, while generation is connected with it and therefore with the field of the accident.

In Book III, 67, Pound follows Aristotle, putting forth the problematic theory of substance as a search for a cause which is separate and One, and for which there is no demonstration: "Di somma importanza sarà la ricerca . . . se oltre la materia esiste, o no, una causa per se; e questa, se sia separata o no, una di numero o più." On 74: "Lo studio verserà intorno alle sostanze, o anche intorno ai loro accidenti? . . . ma non pare che dell'essenza ci sia dimostrazione." On 84: "E come potrà esserci il sapere, se non ci sara qualcosa di unico che si predica di tutti?"

In Book IV, 97, the fundamental definition of metaphysics is offered because the science of being is studied as the universal principle on which all others depend: "C'e una scienza che studia l'essere in quanto essere e la sue proprieta essenziali. Essa è diversa da ognuna delle scienze particolari; poiché nessuna delle altre scienze studia in universale l'essere in quanto essere, ma, dopo averne recisa qualche parte, di questa considera gli accidenti."

In Book VI, 192, Pound follows the peculiarity of the science to which the study of substance belongs, in its being eternal and immobile, as a speculative science: "Ma se qualcosa esiste di eterno immobile e separato, non è dubbio che la conoscenza di esso appartiene a una scienza speculativa." This is the "filosofia prima," that is, the science which studies that which is separate and immobile: "Soltanto la scienza che é prima studia cio che é separato e immobile," and p. 194: "Ma se c'é una sostanza immobile, essa sarà superiore alle altre, e la scienza di essa sarà la prima filosofia."

In Book X, 312, Pound follows the merging of the concept of the One in its being the opposite of the "molteplice": "l'uno e il molteplice si oppongono in moltimodi." In Book XI, 337, the substance is put forth as a guarantee of the order of the world: "Come, se non esistesse un essere eterno e separato e immutabile, ci sarebbe l'ordine nel mondo?"

In Book XII, chap. 8: 396, Pound follows Aristotle's deduction of the concept of perfection from that of immobility: "la natura di ogni sostanza sottratta al mutamento e per se stessa partecipe della perfezione ha valore di fine: nessun'altra natura sarà tale oltre queste. . . ." The problematic being of the divine thinking is taken up on p. 399, where Pound follows Aristotle's focusing on the concept of substance as divine, its peculiarity being immutable thinking and self-sufficiency: "Chiaro é, dunque, ch'essa pensa ciò che v'ha di piu divino e degno di onore, e che il suo pensiero non muta. . . ." This thinking thinks itself: "Esso, dunque, se é cio che v'ha di piu perfetto, pensa se stesso, e l'atto del suo pensiero consiste nel pensamento del suo stesso pensare."

In Book XIV, 468, Pound identifies the cause of the inrooted metaphysics of the West as it emerges from Aristotle's identification of the good with the One. In reference to "alcuni dicono che l'uno in se é il bene in se: la sua sostanza, tuttavia, pensavano che fosse soprattutto quella di esser uno," Pound writes "Monos versus Pan."

The other aspect Pound follows is that of production ("*poiesis*"), related to the concept of nature, set forth by Aristotle in Book V, chap. 4: 144, "Natura si dice, in un senso, la genesi delle cose che hanno un lor crescimento (come se uno pronunziasse lungo l'y di physis)." On p. 146, Pound reads the concept of nature as the substance of those beings which have in themselves the principle of movement (Book V, chap. 4: 10), and for that containing the principle of generation and growth. In Book VI, 190: "la scienza fisica . . . la sostanza ch'essa studia ě quella che ha in se il principio del movimento e dell'inerzia." On p. 191, it is evident that Pound sees physics as the opposite of the science of metaphysics: "la Fisica sarǎ una scienza speculativa, ma speculativa di un essere tale che ha la potenza di muoversi, e della sostanza tratta soltanto secondo nozioni che valgono per lo piu, non separata della materia." On p. 192: "Infatti la fisica studia ciò che esiste separatamente, ma non é immobile. . . .'"

Chapter 7 of Book VII, 22, is of great importance. Here, the concept of Becoming is placed in relation to what is generated by nature or produced by art (*technê*): "Cio che diviene o é generato dalla natura o é prodotto dall'arte . . . La generazione é naturale quando e di cose il cui prodursi a opera di natura." On p. 225, Pound marks Aristotle's distinction between production and generation: "In questo modo, dunque, avvengono le generazioni per natura; le altre si chiamano, propriamente, produzioni. E queste, tutte, son opera o dell'arte o di una facolta o del raziocinio." Carlini's annotation to "*produzioni*" gives the corresponding Greek word: "*poieseis*" (p. 225). On the same page, a crucial concept is that of production as it occurs in art (*technê*): "Dall'arte . . . son prodotte quelle cose di cui la specie ě nell'anima di chi le fa." On p. 226, the relationship is set forth between production and thinking: "pensando, arriva a quell'ultimo termine che ě in suo potere di produrre. (. . .) Il divenire e il movimento consiste, in parte, di pensiero, in parte, di produzione. . . ." Here, Pound mostly follows the concept that the process of making is also the process of thinking, and the process of nature is similar in certain aspects to the process of thinking.

16 Tim Redman, *Ezra Pound and Italian Fascism* (New York: Cambridge University Press, 1991), 221.

17 Guido Cavalcanti, *Rime* (Genoa: Marsano; reprt. in *Make It New*, 345–407), contains a translation of the canzone *Donna me prega* ("Donna mi priega" according to Pound's text). Pound's commentary (p. 389) quotes Carlini's edition of the *Metaphysics*, so it may be deduced that Pound read this book in the 1920s. From the reading marks in the book, it may be hypothesized that Pound in this quotation was using Carlini's *Introduzione alla Metafisica* (see n. 15 above). Apparently, the

reading of Aristotle's *De Anima* (selections ed. Vito Fazio Allmayer [Bari: 1925]; no reading marks) belongs to the same period, the second half of the 1920s.

    The Averroistic commentary to Cavalcanti's *Donna me prega*, made by Dino del Garbo, a Florentine doctor who lived in the fourteenth century, must also be situated within Aristotelianism and mostly within Averroism, and Del Garbo's commentary is the main source for understanding Pound's interpretation of Cavalcanti. For an initial insight into the complex knot of Pound's reading of Cavalcanti in light of Aristotle and medieval Aristotelianism, see Maria Luisa Ardizzone, "La sapienza del sensibile: Pound (Cavalcanti) Aristotele: Prolegomena," *Galleria* 25, nos. 3–6 (1986): 155–182; and "The Genesis and Structure of Pound's Paradise: Looking at the Vocabulary," *Paideuma* 22, no. 3, 1964, pp. 121–168.

18   This last meaning, i.e., of the division between sense and intellect, which points out the dramatic nature of love in Cavalcanti's canzone — has been emphasized by the Italian medievalist Bruno Nardi ("L'Averroismo del primo amico di Dante," *Studi danteschi* 25 [1960]). On Cavalcanti *Donna me prega* see Maria Corti, *La Felicitá Mentale: Nuove prospettive su Dante e Cavalcanti* (Turin: Einaudi, 1982).

19   "But in the history between the XII and the XX centuries, 'evil is' concentrated in Usury/see cantos 45/51, reiterated." This is a fragment, written in the 1940s, of Pound's scheme of the *Cantos*. Originally written in Italian and left unpublished, the text has been inserted in the *Commentary* in the Italian edition of the *Cantos* (*I Cantos*, ed. Mary de Rachewiltz, commentary by Rachewiltz and Maria Luisa Ardizzone [Milan: Mondadori, 1985], 1565–1566). For trans., see Maria Luisa Ardizzone, "The Genesis and Structure of Pound's Paradise: Looking at the Vocabulary," *Paideuma* 22, no. 3 (1996), pp. 121–148.

20   The same historical necessity motivated the theory of updating and fitting style to thought pointed out by Erasmus of Rotterdam in his *Ciceronianus*. In the humanist Lorenzo Valla's *Elegantiae*, the polemic against logic displays a similar viewpoint. Valla's *Elegantiae*, which Pound variously recalls in the 1910s, occupies a crucial position in the *Ur-Cantos*. See *Three Cantos*, I, II, III (1917), reprt. in rev. ed. of *Personae* (New York: New Directions, 1990), prepared by Lea Baechler and A. Walton Litz. Erasmus is recalled in "Renaissance" (1914), (*Literary Essays*, 220), in which Pound quotes Valla's *Elegantiae*.

21   See in particular *How to Write*, 73; *Addenda*, 83; *Debabelization and Ogden*, 103; and *Pragmatic Aesthetics*, 133.

22   During the Middle Ages, poetry was associated with the arts of trivium (that is, grammar, dialectic, and rhetoric). For an introduction to these themes see Ernst Robert Curtius, *European Literature and the Latin Middle Ages* (1953; Princeton, N.J.: Princeton University Press, 1990), esp. chaps. 3, 6, and 8.

23   See "Affirmations: Analysis of This Decade," in *Gaudier-Brzeska*, 111–117; and "The Renaissance" (1914), in *Literary Essays*, 214–226.

24   This appears to be enunciated as problematic in *Ur-Cantos* I: "I stand before the booth, the speech, this booth is full of the marrow of wisdom" (*Personae* [1990], 229).

25   *Gaudier-Brzeska*, 113.

26 Giovanni Gentile, *Studi Vichiani* (Bari: Laterza, 1927), (PB). Gentile was an eminent philosopher and minister of education during the 1920s Fascist years. He was killed by partisans 15 April 1944. Pound recalls Gentile in *Rock-Drill* 89: 599.

27 Francis Bacon, *Novum Organum*, trans. R. Ellis and J. Spedding, intro. R. L. Ellis (New York: E. P. Dutton, n.d.), with a notation on the front page "Ezra Pound, Rapallo," PB.

28 G. W. Leibniz, *Nouveaux Essais sur l'entendement humain* (Paris: Flammarion, n.d.), PB.

29 From his reading marks it can be deduced that Pound read *Studi Vichiani* at different times. One of Pound's notes in the book indicates that he was reading it on "April 15, XXIII (1945)."

30 Pound's edition of Bacon's *Novum Organum* contains reading marks that appear to be made on two separate occasions, or along two different lines of thought. From one angle, Pound follows Bacon's polemic against logic and his attempt to establish the new science of nature, followed by what appears to be Pound's penciled reading marks, which he makes beginning with Bacon's preface (p. 55): "Those who have taken upon them to lay down the law of nature as a thing already searched out and understood, whether they have spoken in simple assurance, or professional affectation, have therein done philosophy and the sciences great injury." Other important reading marks are the ones shaded in Book I to aphorisms XII ("The logic now in use serves rather to fix and give stability to the errors which have their foundation in commonly received notions than to help the search after truth . . .), to LI ("Human understanding is of its own nature prone to abstractions and gives a substance and reality to things which are fleeting . . ."), to LIV ("Aristotle made his natural philosophy a mere bond servant to his logic"), and to LXIII ("Aristotle who corrupted natural philosophy by his logic . . . fashioning the world out of categories"). The second line of thought is grasped by means of blue-penciled reading marks. They appear to follow Bacon's concept of form through the following aphorisms: Book I, aphorism LI, and Book II, aphorisms II, IV, XVI, XVII. I quote from Book I, aphorism LI: "It is best to consider matters, its conformation and the changes of that conformation, its own action, and the law of this action or motion; for *forms are a mere fiction of the human mind, unless you will call the laws of action by that name*" (emphasis mine). And from Book II, aphorism II: "Nor have I forgotten that in a former passage I noted and corrected as an error of the human mind the opinion that Forms give existence. For though in nature nothing really exists beside individual bodies, performing pure individual acts according to a fixed law, yet in philosophy this very law, and the investigation, discovery, and explanation of it, is the foundation as well of knowledge as of operation. And it is this law, with its clauses, that I mean when I speak of *Forms;* a name which I'd rather adopt because it has grown into use and become familiar."

31 Pound's edition of Leibniz's *Nouveaux essais* contained a minor Leibniz text, "Sur une réforme de la philosophie première et sur la notion de substance" (pp. 490–492). As was his customary practice with books he was reading, Pound wrote down page numbers in the back, and here p. 492 is mentioned twice. Leibniz's "Sur une

réforme . . ." focuses on criticism of the concept of substance. Opposing the Aristotelian, Scholastic, and Cartesian notions, Leibniz proposes substance as force. I
quote some passages as marked by Pound:

> Pour en donner un avant-goût, je dirai en passant que la notion de *force* (en
> allemand *kraft*, en latin *virtus*), au développement de laquelle je destine une sci-
> ence spéciale, la *dynamique*, jette le plus grand jour sur la notion de substance.
> La force active ou agissante n'est pas la puissance nue de l'école, il ne faut pas
> l'entendre en effet, ainsi que les scolastiques, comme une simple faculté ou pos-
> sibilité d'agir, qui pour être effectuée ou réduite à l'acte, aurait besoin d'une
> excitation venue du dehors, et comme d'un *stimulus* étranger. La véritable force
> active renferme l'action en elle-même; elle est *entéléchie*, pouvoir moyen entre
> la simple faculté d'agir et l'acte determiné ou effectué, elle contient et enveloppe
> l'effort; elle se détermine d'elle-même à l'action, et n'a pas besoin d'y être aidée,
> mais seulement de n'être pas empêchée. L'exemple d'un poids qui tend la corde
> à laquelle il est suspendu, ou celui d'un arc tendu, peut éclaircir cette notion.
> En effet, bien que la gravité ou la force d'élasticité puissent et doivent être ex-
> pliquées mécaniquement par le mouvement de l'éther, néanmoins la dernière
> raison du mouvement dans la matière est la force déposée dans la création, mise
> en chaque corps, mais limitée et empêchée diversement dans la nature par le
> conflit des corps. *Et cette puissance d'agir, je dis qu'elle est dans toute substance*
> [emphasis mine], et qu'il en nait toujours, quelque action; au point que ni la sub-
> stance spirituelle, ni même la substance corporelle, ne cesse jamais d'agir; et c'est
> ce que ne paraissent pas avoir assex compris ceux qui ont fait consister l'essence
> des corps ou dans la seule extension ou même dans l'impénétrabilité. . . .

32   *ABC of Reading*, 17 and 26. Leibniz's concept of "comparison" and/or "relation" as
an operation of human understanding is followed by Pound mostly through Book
II, xi, 4–6, of *Nouveaux essais*. I quote:

> §4. PHILALETHE. Une autre opération de l'ésprit à l'égard de ses idées, c'est la
> *comparaison* qu'il fait d'une idée avec l'autre par rapport à l'étendue, aux de-
> grés, au temps, au lieu, ou à quelque autre circonstance: c'est de là que dépend
> ce grand nombre d'idées qui sont comprises sous le nom de *relation*.
> THÉOPHILE. [Selon mon sens la relation est plus generale que la comparaison.
> Car les *relations* sont ou de *comparaison* ou de *concours*. Les premières regar-
> dent la *convenance* ou *disconvenance* (je prends ces termes dans un sens moins
> large), qui comprend la ressemblance, l'égalité, l'inégalité, etc. Les secondes ren-
> ferment quelque *liaison*, comme de la cause et de l'effet, du tout et des parties,
> de la situation et de l'ordre, etc.]

33   The idea that thought is a combinatorial activity is marked by Pound throughout
Book II of *Nouveaux essais*. I quote from chap. XI:

> §6. PHILALETHE. La *composition* des idées simples, pour en faire des complexes,
> est encore une opération de notre esprit. On peut rapporter à cela la faculté
> d'*étendre les idées*, en joignant ensemble celles qui sont d'une même espèce,
> comme en formant une douzaine de plusieurs unités.

THÉOPHILE. [L'un est aussi bien composé que l'autre sans doute; mais la composition des idées semblables n'est plus simple que celle des idées différentes.]

34   Leo Frobenius's Paideuma proposes the idea of culture as an organic whole and the idea of an organicity among the cultures. I cite a fragment by Frobenius, *An Anthology* (Wiesbaden: F. Steiner, 1973), 43, in which he explains the meaning of the word "Paideuma": "As I have argued elsewhere, cultural manifestations are to be regarded as expressions of an organic unity which is not something man-made so much as something that imposes itself on men. We call this 'culture,' but the term is too vague and hackneyed on the one hand and too specific on the other. For this reason, and to express something both broader and deeper, I adopted the term 'Paideuma.' This may be described as a substantive entity with its own laws of development [. . . .]" In "For a New Paideuma," in *Selected Prose*, 284, Pound uses the term "complex" to render this idea of culture as an organic whole (see n. 44 below). Pound's correspondence with the Frobenius Institute (BRBL) informs us that Pound tried to find an English publisher for Frobenius's *Paideuma;* that is, vol. 4 of Frobenius, *Erlebte Erdteile*, 7 vols. (Frankfurt am Main: n.p., 1925–1929).

35   Gentile, *Studi Vichiani*, 118. This quotation is from Vico's "orazione," "De antiquissima Italorum Sapientia," in which Vico focused on the concept of the coincidence between doing and knowing. This concept announces Vico's well-known idea of history as science (*Scienza nuova*). That is, history is that which has been made by man. History is science because man can know only what he himself has made. For Vico, history and art are *technê*.

36   "Se la scienza della natura è offuscata dall'ignoranza ineliminabile dell'interno processo della natura. . . ." (If the science of nature is dimmed by the unavoidable ignorance of the inner process of nature . . .) G. Gentile, *Studi Vichiani* (Bari: Latezza, 1922), 128.

37   Rémy de Gourmont's *Physique de l'amour* (1903), trans. with postscript by Pound as *The Natural Philosophy of Love* (New York: Boni and Liveright, 1922), has to be considered an important step in Pound's reflection on biological logic. (I explain the connection in the second part of my introduction.) About Gourmont, Pound wrote: "*Physique de l'amour* (1903) should be used as textbook of biology" (*Instigations*, 174). For the importance of Pound's relationship to Gourmont see Richard Sieburth, *Instigations: Ezra Pound and Rémy de Gourmont* (Cambridge, Mass.: Harvard University Press, 1978).

38   "*Technê:* Art, skill, cunning of hand; an art or craft, i.e., a set of rules, system or method of making or doing." Liddell-Scott, *Greek-English Dictionary*, PB. Aristotle, *Nicomachaean Ethics*, VI, iv: 3–4, defines *technê* as "skill in making . . . rational quality concerned with making." In the 1930s, Pound dedicated forty pages of *Guide to Kulchur* (1938) to reading and commentary on the *Nicomachaean Ethics*, in Henry Racham's ed. of *Guide to Kulchur* (New York: New Directions, 1952), 304–349. There, *technê* is defined by Pound as "skill as an art, in making things" (p. 327). Aristotle's concept of *technê* is also contained, among the books Pound read, in the *Metaphysics*. We know that Pound read an abridged edition of the *Metaphysics* in

the second half of the 1920s because he recalled it in his commentary on Cavalcanti (see nn. 15 and 17 above). Plato's *Cratylus* proposes *technê* as habit of mind. This appears to be most important for Pound from the late 1930s on. In *Republic X: 23*, the value, perfection, beauty of a thing is defined in relation to the concept of function; that is, beauty corresponds to the utility for which a thing is made. In the same book, the work of the *artifex* is highly prized, while the imitative arts, such as painting and poetry, are devalued. This tradition was highly important in medieval culture, particularly for the Chartres school.

39 For art as *technê* in Greek culture see W. Tatarkiewicz, *History of Aesthetics*, 3 vols. (The Hague: Mouton, 1970), 1: 25–30, 138–141; and *A History of Six Ideas: An Essay on Aesthetics* (The Hague: Martinus Nijhoff, 1980), 11–15, 50–56, 73–83.

40 "How to Read" (1929), in *Literary Essays*, 15–40.

41 Pound is reticent about the meaning he gives to "logopoeia." In "How to Read" (p. 25), he proposes that "logopoeia" is "the dance of the intellect among words . . . it holds the aesthetic content which is peculiarly the domain of verbal manifestation." A few lines later he asserts, "Logopoeia does not translate." The meaning I propose is the literal translation of the Greek roots "*logos*" (word) and "*poeio*" (to make).

42 In "How to Read" (p. 29), Pound explains that "the problem we started with" is that of "the art of writing, the art of charging language with meaning." "Great Literature" is defined as "language charged with meaning to the utmost possible degree" (p. 23). This statement is recalled in *ABC of Reading*, 28.

43 Fenollosa's pivotal idea that the ideogram carries things onto the page comes from Leibniz. In the *Nouveaux Essais* (underlined by Pound in his notes), we read: "Les Chinois n'ont-ils pas comme nous des sons articulés? Et cependant s'étant attachés à une autre manière d'écrire, ils ne se sont pas encore avisés de faire un alphabet de ces sons. C'est aussi qu'on possède bien des choses sans le savoir." I encountered the first insight about this relationship between Fenollosa and Leibniz in Hugh Kenner, *The Pound Era* (Berkeley: University of California Press, 1971).

44 For the edition of Aristotle in Pound's library, see n. 15 above. Pound's reading marks focus on chap. X, 1–3 ("Unity and Other General Attributes of Substance").

45 Pound's idea of culture as Paideuma is crucial for understanding his virulent antiSemitism from the 1930s onward and for his treatment of aesthetics. Frobenius's idea that there is a connection between, for instance, the form of a bed which certain people make and use and the kind of economy (agricultural and sedentary, or nomadic) (see Frobenius, *Anthology*, 9) is crucial for Pound's idea that an economy of usury will influence art: "form." Pound summarizes this idea in a single assertion, variously reiterated: "The form of objects is due to CAUSE" (see letters to Fox, in Appendix p. xxx). In *Guide to Kulchur*, 57, Pound explains the meaning of "Paideuma" as follows: "To escape a word or a set of words loaded up with dead association Frobenius uses the term 'Paideuma' for the single or *complex* of the inrooted ideas of any period." In "For a New Paideuma," he writes: "The term 'Paideuma' as used in a dozen German volumes has been given the sense of an active element in the era, the *complex* of ideas which is in a given time germinal, reaching into the next epoch, but *conditioning actively all the thought and action of its*

own time" (*Selected Prose*, 284; emphasis mine). I have stressed the importance of the word "complex," which in Pound's work belongs to the idea of a unity that is one and plural.

46 Pound utilizes the words "monotheism" and "monism" as synonymous. However, the word "monism" includes a different meaning from Pound's. Pound stresses the root "monos," common to both words, and in this sense, "monism" appears to be applied broadly. According to the *Macmillan Encyclopedia of Philosophy*'s entry on "Monism and Pluralism": "In the nineteenth century the word 'monism' came to be given wider application and so to have a systematic ambiguity, that is, a consistent variation of meaning according to context. Since then any theory that tries to reduce all phenomena to a single principle, or to explain them by one principle . . . has been labeled 'monism.'" I am indebted to Professor Leon Surette for calling my attention to the necessity of clarifying this issue.

47 In his critique of monism Pound seems mostly to follow Leibniz's criticism of Spinoza as formulated mainly in a book edited in the nineteenth century, *A Refutation of Spinoza by Leibniz*, with prefatory remarks and intro. by Foucher de Careil, trans. O. F. Owen (London: Hamilton, Adams, 1855). T. S. Eliot cited this book in an essay on Leibniz ("The Development of Leibniz's Monadism," *Monist* [1916]), reprt. Eliot, *Knowledge and Experience in the Philosophy of F. R. Bradley* (New York: Harcourt, Brace and Co., 1964), 177–197. Leibniz's criticism of Spinoza was strictly theoretical and implied no anti-Semitism; Spinoza, who lived in Holland, was descended from Spanish Jews.

48 Pound had inserted a text by Voltaire ("Genesis") into *Instigations* (1920). "Genesis" begins with a consideration of the reduction of the plural gods present in the Phoenician source to the One. I quote some fragments: " 'In the beginning God created heaven and earth,' that is the way they translate it, yet there is scarcely any one so ignorant as not to know that the original reads 'the gods create heaven and hearth' which reading conforms to the Phoenician idea that God employed lesser divinities to untangle chaos . . . the inspired author bows to the vague and stupid prejudice of his nation. . . . The Bible shows continuous ignorance of nature in which reason and decent custom are outraged in every page" (266, 268).

49 I found no trace of this connection in relatively recent books proposing an interpretation of Pound's anti-Semitism, such as, Robert Casillo, *The Genealogy of Demons* (Evanston, Ill.: Northwestern University Press, 1988), or Wendy Flory, *The American Ezra Pound* (New Haven, Conn.: Yale University Press, 1988), both of which contain sections dedicated to Pound's anti-Semitism. Instead, scholars recognize the connection between monotheism and usury. In *Ezra Pound: Idee Fondamentali, 1931–1943*, ed. Caterina Ricciardi (Rome: 1990), a collection of Pound's articles published in the Italian newspaper *Meridiano di Roma*, I found that Pound did not reiterate this connection between language and Hebrew monotheism.

50 Ernest Renan, *Averroé et l'Averroïsme* (1892), is one of the sources of Pound's interpretation of Cavalcanti (*Make It New*, 356–407), where it is mentioned on pp. 386–389.

51 The Renan writing is contained in Book VIII of *Oeuvres Complètes* (Paris:

Calmann-Lévy, 1947–1961) and was first published in the 1850s. Renan's study on Semitic language is assumed to be responsible for "rational anti-Semitism." See H. Coudenhove-Kalergi, *Anti-Semitism Throughout the Ages* (London: 1901), 36–39. In Renan's studies, many of his viewpoints are similar to Pound's. In the preface to the 1858 edition, Renan declares that one of his goals is to make precise "the notion of the monotheism of Semites" (p. 132). In Book 1, chap. 1, Renan attributes to Semitic peoples the negative characteristic of being nomad and monotheist (p. 140), of lacking the sense of nature (p. 148), of lacking mythology (p. 148). For Renan, Semitic people have no science or philosophy (p. 144), nor do they have the sense of manyness (pp. 146, 156). The poetry expressed by this race is totally lacking in creative imagination (p. 151). Semitic people have no plastic arts (p. 152) or epics. "La grande épopée sort toujours d'une mythologie. Elle n'est pas possible qu'avec la lutte des élements divines . . . mais que faire pour l'épopée de ce Jehovah solitaire, qui est celui qui est?" (pp. 152–153). I recall all of these peculiarities because Renan puts them in relation to language. Language being a document of the consciousness of a people (p. 134), Semitic peoples have a specific language, and the peculiarities of this language correspond to the peculiarities of the people who spoke, used, and were limited by that language: "Il faut dire, ce semble, que dans l'état actuel de la science, les langues sémitiques doivent être envisagés comme correspondant à une division du genre humain; en effet, le caractère du peuples que les ont parlées est marqué dans l'histoire par des traits aussi originaux que les langues qui ont servi de formule et de limite à leur pensée" (p. 144). It should be pointed out that in Renan, Semitic people included Arabic people.

52   This denunciation is variously reiterated by Pound beginning at the end of the 1930s. See particularly, *The Letters of Ezra Pound: 1907–1941*, ed. D. D. Paige (New York: Harcourt, Brace & Co., 1950), the letter of 1940 to George Santayana, p. 333 (see n. 115 for quotation); a letter of the same year to T. S. Eliot, p. 336; and "Addenda 1952," in *Guide to Kulchur*, 351. In "Mang Tse" (1938), *Selected Prose*, 86, we read: "Aristotle . . . began his list of mental processes with *technê*, and the damned college parrots omitted it."

53   John McCormick, *George Santayana: A Biography* (New York: Knopf, 1987), 399–400.

54   Pound's correspondence with Santayana, partially unpublished and preserved in BRBL and in HRHR, has been crucial to my reconstruction of the section "European *Paideuma*" because of the insistence reiterated in these letters in considering the connection among language, knowledge, and religion. The correspondence between the themes of the "European *Paideuma*" section and the contents of the letters to Santayana of the same years (1940–1942) is important principally because these topics, as discussed in these letters, are related to Pound's project to write a new section of the poem after that of *Cantos* LII–LXXI.

55   *The Chinese Written Character*, 441–450. Pound's notes, which contain his study of some ideograms, were introduced by: "Fenollosa left the notes unfinished; I am proceeding in ignorance and by conjecture. The primitive pictures were 'squared' at certain times."

56   In *Vorticism*, Pound writes that Euclidean geometry "does not *create* form . . . statements in plane or descriptive geometry are like talk about art. They are criticism of the form. The form is not created by them." To Euclidean geometry is thus opposed the analytical geometry of Descartes and the new conception of space. In relation to such a cognitive level, Pound explains that the term "Vortex" derives from the necessity of giving a name to these new types of relations and extends to poetry the relations set forth concerning painting and sculpture: "It is as true for painting and sculpture as it is for the poetry" (*Gaudier-Brzeska*, 92). In *Pragmatic Aesthetics*, Pound predates to *Vorticism* this relation between writing and mathematics. Nevertheless, in *Vorticism*, the relation that was proposed was not so clearly bound to writing as it was to the arts in general. It may be held nevertheless that somehow Pound had attributed to those years a clarity of perspective that was won at a later date.

57   Hans Reichenbach, *The Rise of Scientific Philosophy* (Berkeley: University of California Press, 1951); Werner Heisenberg, *Physics and Philosophy: The Revolution in Modern Science* (New York: Harper and Row, 1962).

58   Fenollosa's essay, *The Chinese Written Character*, is a masterpiece of criticism on grammar (with particular emphasis on the grammar of the English language) in its derivation from the logic of syllogism. Fenollosa's statements, such as "Logic has abused the language . . . nature itself has not grammar" (20), explain that such opposition is an attempt to substitute the laws of nature for those of grammar and syllogism.

59   *ABC of Reading*, 17–27.

60   Galileo Galilei, "Il saggiatore," in *Opere*, ed. F. Flora (Milan-Naples: Ricciardi, 1953), 33. Pound recalls Galileo in *ABC of Reading*, 20: "for having stopped to discuss about things and had begun to look at them, and to invent means (like the telescope) of seeing them better," and in *Guide to Kulchur*, 50. In Canto 85, "Galileo indexed 1616" is connected to the ideogram of Sun.

61   "Science developed more rapidly after Bacon had suggested the direct examination of phenomena." *ABC of Reading*, 10.

62   This article was a review of C. K. Ogden's *Debabelization (With a Survey of Contemporary Opinion on the Problem of a Universal Language)*, pub. as no. 36 of the Psyche series (London: Kegan, Trench, Trubner, 1931). Ogden's Basic English proposed the selection of 850 English words for use as a basic vocabulary. The Pound-Ogden relation is documented in their correspondence and preserved in the Beinecke Rare Book Library. Pound's ideogrammic series was planned to oppose Ogden's Basic English. Traces of this opposition are in Pound's foreword (p. 5) to the 1936 ed. of Fenollosa's *The Chinese Written Character*.

63   This is an allusion to Julien Benda, *Le trahison des clercs* (n.p., 1927).

64   Pound's continuous references to the relationship between literature and science start by the 1910s. However, it is from the late 1920s that he concentrates on the attempt to bring into literature the results of science. For the relevance of Pound's connection with science see Ian Bell, *The Critic as Scientist* (New York: Methuen, 1981).

65   *Instigations* (1920), 357–388.

66   This historical sense in *Vortex* (1914) leads Pound to focus on the importance of the past, counteracting Marinetti's Futurism. For Pound, the future will arise only from an understanding of the experience of the past, while for Futurism it is the past tradition that mostly needs to be exorcised: "All the energized past, all the past that is living and worthy to live . . . all the past that is vital, all the past that is capable of living into the future, is pregnant into the vortex now." *Ezra Pound and the Visual Arts*, 151.

67   *The Little Review*, a New York literary magazine, was founded and directed by Margaret Anderson. In the 1920s, under the new leadership of Jane Heap, the magazine focused on the debate on the arts, and in 1927 it organized a Machine Age Exposition between 16 May and 28 May. The issue published for the exhibition contained articles on machines and architecture and a relevant panorama of European and American architecture and art, with photographic documentation. The lead editorial was written by Heap. Among the contributions an article by the Italian Futurist Enrico Prampolini contained a reiteration of the Futurists' position on machines. The catalog focused mostly on architecture and industrial architecture but also on machines, including some pictures by artists. Among the architects represented were Le Corbusier and Gropius, and among the artists were Archipenko, Duchamp, and Man Ray. The cover featured a reproduction of a work by Fernand Léger.

68   The word "art" is the English translation of the Latin *ars*, which translated the Greek *technê* ("*Technê*: an art or craft, i.e., a set of rules, a system of regular methods of making or doing . . . whether of the useful arts or of the fine arts" Liddell-Scott, *Greek-English Dictionary*, PB). In Western civilization the two terms had a separate evolution, while in Greece the word *technê* contained both technical and artistic meaning. During the Middle Ages the word "art" also had a broadening meaning, since it encompassed handicrafts, sciences, and the fine arts. All medieval definitions of art agree that art is a ruled skill to make something. Hugh of St. Victor writes in *Didascalicon:* "Ars potest dici scientia quae in artis praeceptis regulisque consistit." On art in the medieval age see Edgar De Bruyne, *Etudes d'Esthétique Medievale*, 3 vols. (Geneva: Slatkine Reprints, 1975), esp. 2: 371–420; for *technê* in Greek civilization see Tatarkiewicz, *A History of Six Ideas*, 56–57 and 78–83.

69   For an introduction to the origins of the relationship which in the history of aesthetics connects the concept of form (conceived as an ideal and perfect form) to the sphere of Platonism and metaphysics, see Erwin Panofsky, *Idea: A Concept in Art Theory* (New York: Columbia University Press, 1968), esp. 3–43. See also Tatarkiewicz, *A History of Six Ideas*, 220–243.

70   For "aptness to purpose" as a recurring aesthetic principle in the history of art see E. A. De Zurko, *Origins of Functionalism* (New York: Knopf, 1957).

71   For the relationship between Pound's *Vortex* and Futurism see Marjorie Perloff, *The Futurist Moment: Avant-Garde, Avant-Guerre, and the Language of Rupture* (Chicago: University of Chicago Press, 1986), esp. 163–193. Pound's relationship to the Bauhaus must be considered in light of *Machine Art*. Functionalism was for the

most part a Bauhaus proposal. Also, the relationship between art and technique was a point of view proposed mostly by the Bauhaus. To the Bauhaus's emphasis on architecture, Pound counterposed the machine. More than Gropius, Pound's position is close to that of Kandinsky and Paul Klee, both of whom joined the Bauhaus in the 1920s. These artists' emphasis on exact investigation and the importance they give for art to studies in algebra, geometry, and mechanics appear to be close to Pound's. See H. Bayer, B. Gropius, and I. Gropius, eds., *Bauhaus, 1919–1928* (New York: Museum of Modern Art, 1938; rpt. 1986), esp. material on Klee's courses (pp. 37, 170) and Kandinsky's courses (pp. 38, 168–169).

72   Fernand Léger, "The Aesthetics of the Machine, Manufactured Objects, Artisan and Artist," *The Little Review* (1923-1924). Pound does not take into account Léger's emphasis on manufactured objects. The text of Léger's article was a lecture given in the Collège de France, Paris, in 1923. Pound's knowledge of the Bauhaus could be related to his years in Paris.

73   "Form in music is TIME . . . as I said before the stuff of which music is made is not sound-vibration, but TIME." George Antheil, "Time in Abstraction and Music," *The Little Review* (Autumn 1924–Winter 1925), dedicated to Juan Gris.

74   "I use the term 'great bass' to designate the frequencies below those which the ear has been accustomed to consider as 'notes.'" For an introduction to the concept of "great bass" in Pound see R. Murray Shafer, ed., *Ezra Pound and Music* (New York: New Directions, 1977), 467–480. However, Shaffer's important book does not take into account Pound's explanation of "great bass" as contained in *Machine Art*.

75   For Pound's relationship between art and economics (which influenced his view of the machine), reference should be made to Pound's relationship with Alfred Orage. See Martin Wallace, *The New Age Under Orage: Chapters in English Cultural History* (Manchester: University of Manchester Press, 1967), and Redman, *Ezra Pound and Italian Fascism*, 17–50. For Pound's relationship with C. H. Douglas see Redman, 50–75.

76   "ABC of Economics" (1933), in *Selected Prose*, 233.

77   In Canto 51, which contains the reiteration of Canto 45 against usury, Pound opposes to usury the *technê* of fishing: "Blue dun; number 2 in most rivers / for dark days; when it is cold / A starling's wing will give you the colour . . . ." The source of this technique is in a book of instructions for fishermen, Charles Bowkler's *The Art of Angling* (1829), PB. I am recalling this canto because in it appears the idea of *technê* in its oppositional relation to usury, similar to the one I am proposing, that is, *technê* allowing the possibility to make use of the abundance of nature.

78   On the basis of the correspondence with the vendors of machines who provided Pound with photographic material, I would deduce that *Machine Art* was planned as an essay on "American art." (Mary de Rachewiltz provided me with some letters written from vendors to Homer Pound, the poet's father, who helped him collect photographs. In this correspondence, references are made to an essay on "American art.")

79   "Patria Mia" (1913), in *Selected Prose*, 101–141.

80 BRBL Folder: "Definitions," 4436. This emphasis on economics can also show that, by 1931, Pound had lost interest in the machine. His brief note to *The New Review* (1931) should be explained mostly in this light.

81 Aristotle, *Metaphysics* VII, 7: 3–6; and *Nicomachaean Ethics* VI, 4: 4.

82 "But if you will follow this process . . . plus always *technê*," *Cantos*, 85: 430.

83 "N.B. Usury: A charge for the use of purchasing power, levied without regard to production; often without regard to the possibilities of production . . ." *Canto 45*, 310. Pound's concept of usury, seen as an opposition to production (in its inner relationship to generation), echoes Aristotle's definition of "usury" as given in *Politics*. Pound's copy is in HRHR; trans. H. Rackham (New York: G. P. Putnam's, 1932). I quote a passage which Pound has marked: "Usury . . . is most reasonably hated because its gain comes from money itself and not from that for the sake of which money was invented. For money was brought into existence for the purpose of exchange, but interest increases the amount of the money itself and this is the actual origin of the Greek word: offspring resembles parent, and interest is money born of money; consequently this form of the business of getting wealth is of all forms the most contrary to nature" (51).

84 "My subject is poetry not language, yet the roots of poetry are in language." Fenollosa, *The Chinese Written Character*, 10.

85 What Pound wrote in *Guide to Kulchur*, 74, about the Leibnizian monad explains that he sees in it the prefiguration of the nature of matter as discovered in the scientist's laboratory. "Leibniz was the last philosopher who 'got hold something,' his unsquashable *monad* may be now have been pulverized into *sub-electrons*, it may have been magnified in the microscope's eye to the elaborate structure of a solar system, but it holds as a concept." Leibniz's explanation of his monad as given in his correspondence with Bossuet ("qu'il n'y a point de portion de matière si petite dans laquelle il n'y ait un monde infini de créatures") (Bossuet, *Correspondance*, ed. C. H. Urbain and B. Lévesque [Paris: Hachette, 1912], vol. 5) suggests the meaning of "monad" that Pound will emphasize. The reference (in "The Jefferson-Adams Letters as a Shrine and a Monument" [1937–1938], in *Selected Prose*, 156) to the Leibniz-Bossuet correspondence shows that Pound, in denouncing here the devaluation of philosophy in light of material science, is referring to Leibniz's definition of "monad" as given in this correspondence.

86 The draft is contained in Folder 3595 ("How to Read: Notes") and entitled "Categories": "The categories of literary and poetry criticism have remained mostly those of the Greek critics . . . in any case I offer a different lot: melopoeia; the musical property of the word. Phanopoeia: casting of images on the imagination and a third property which may be called logopoeia, or a play and shading or 'dance' of the words themselves; the part of the art that is of the language and is shared by no other art."

87 "*Poeio:* used in two general senses, 'make' and 'do.' Make, produce . . . After Homer of Poets" (Liddell-Scott, *Greek-English Dictionary*, PB). At the end of the 1920s, Pound was reading Aristotle's *On the Art of Poetry*, trans. Ingram Bywater, with

a preface by G. Murray (Oxford: Clarendon Press, 1929), PB. The book's preface underlined this meaning of *poeiō*, "to make."

88 Plato still sometimes uses "poiesis" and "poietes" in the broader sense of any production or any producer. Plato, *Symposium*, 205 C, and *Phaedrus*, 234 E. In Aristotle's *Metaphysics* VII, 7, the activity of intelligence is *poiesis*: production. See n. 15 above.

89 This relationship appears to be suggested most often in the section *Addenda*, where it is put forth as between "art as biology" and "logic as biological" and the coincidence between the nature of matter and that of mind. These relationships suggest a homology between the processes of nature and those of thought and language, which comprise poetry and art. That is, art and poetry do not imitate nature because they are, in fact, part of the process of nature.

90 See n. 6 above, and Gallup, *A Bibliography*, 452.

91 Postscript to *The Natural Philosophy of Love* by Rémy de Gourmont" is now contained in *Pavannes and Divagations* (New York: New Directions, 1958), 203–214. This postscript, which is important for an explanation of Pound's idea of intelligence and the relationship he establishes between brain activity and imaginative activity, is the first document to reconstruct his idea that what presides over so-called artistic activity implies all human intelligence and not simply intuition.

92 In the fragment, "Them 'Eavy Thinkers," pp. 118–19, Pound criticizes Russell. The book to which he refers is Bertrand Russell, *Philosophy* (New York: W. W. Norton, 1929), previously published in England under the title *An Outline of Philosophy* (1927). Pound probably read the English edition.

93 *Literary Essays*, 25.

94 "Collected Prose," Folder 2945, BRBL. "The thesis in my translation of Gourmont's *Physiqué de l'Amour* is worth considering. The skull doesn't hold all the human intelligence."

95 "The brain is also a quintessence, or at least in rapport with all parts of the body." *A Postscript*, 212.

96 "You have the visualizing sense, the 'stretch' of imagination, the mystics . . . Santa Teresa, who saw the microcosmos, hell, heaven, purgatory, complete . . ." *A Postscript*, 211.

97 "Thought is a chemical process in relation to the organ the brain: creative thought is an act like fecundation. . . . The creative thought manifests itself in images, in music, which is to sound what the concrete image is to sight. . . . This hypothesis would perhaps explain a certain number of as yet uncorrelated phenomena both psychological and physiological. It would explain the enormous content of the brain as a *maker or presenter of images*." *A Postscript*, 207–208, 203; emphasis mine.

98 "Phanopoeia, which is the casting of images upon the visual imagination." *How to Read*, 25.

99 "Is not thought precisely a form-comparing and form-combining?" *A Postscript*, p. 207.

100 Fenollosa's *The Chinese Written Character* attacked grammar as deriving from

medieval logic. Metaphysics is indicated by Fenollosa through the term "abstraction." "Of course this view of the grammarians springs from the discredited, or rather the useless, logic of the Middle Ages. According to this logic, thought deals with abstractions, concepts drawn out of things by a sifting process" (Fenollosa, p. 15).

101 According to the Gestaltists, "Gestalt is a whole whose characteristics are determined not by the characteristics of its individual elements, but by the internal nature of the whole." David Katz, *Gestalt Psychology* (New York: Ronald Press, 1950), 91. Gestalt psychology originated in Germany in the 1910s and developed rapidly in the 1920s. In 1925 two authoritative representatives of this school, Wolfgang Kohler and Kurt Koffka, came to the United States for lecture tours and were given temporary academic appointments. In 1929, Kohler's *Gestalt Psychology* was translated into English and published in New York by Liveright. See George W. Hartmann, *Gestalt Psychology: A Survey of Facts and Principles* (New York: Ronald Press, 1935). Pound probably had information about this group from some reviews. What is important for Pound is the concept of the whole, that is, the multiplicity as organic and not as the sum of the parts. The identification of physics and psychology present mostly in Koffka and Kohler seems to be the new field of knowledge which Pound is considering.

102 In "the ideogrammic method or the method of science" (*ABC of Reading*, 26–27), the relationship with science appears to be formulated for the method rather than for the contents of science.

103 In Gestalt psychology, "physics becomes the basic science for psychology as well as other fields" (Katz, *Gestalt Psychology*, 93). The appeal to physics appears evident in Kohler's explanation of the meaning of Gestalt: "In physics, a molecule as a larger functional whole contains several atoms, a subordinate whole. The atoms belong to the molecule functionally; still they do not altogether lose their functional individuality in that dynamical whole" (Kohler, *Gestalt Psychology*, 156–157). In Hartmann, *Gestalt Psychology*, 72, we read: "Gestalt taught psychology to speak the language of 20th-century physics." Hartmann (p. 50) informs us that both Albert Einstein and Kohler were students of Max Planck, and he makes connections between Gestalt psychology and Einsteinian relativity. Among the various sources for Pound's interest in biology, I note that in *Guide to Kulchur* he mentions J. B. S. Haldane, the English biochemist and geneticist.

104 Aristotle, *De Interpretatione*, 16b 20: "verbs in themselves—said alone—are names and signify something."

105 Oswald Spengler's *The Decline of the West* (1918) was translated into English and published in New York by Alfred A. Knopf in the 1920s.

106 Letters to George Santayana, 16 and 21 Nov. 1940; Folder "Santayana, George," 1562, BRBL. See also *Ezra Pound e la scienza*, 46.

107 The editions of Confucius recalled in the radio speech were the Italian translations being published by Pound in Italy at that time: Confucio, *Studio integrale*, versione di E. Pound e Alberto Lucchini (Rapallo: Scuola tipografica orfanatrofio Emiliani, 1942); *Testamento di Confucio*, versione italiana di E. Pound e Alberto Lucchini

(Venice: Casa editrice dell'edizione popolari, 1944); *Chung Young, L'asse che non vacilla*, versione italiana di E. Pound (Venice: Casa editrice dell'edizione popolari, 1945). For the English translations see *Confucius: The Great Digest, The Unwobbling Pivot, The Analects*, trans. and commentary by Ezra Pound (New York: New Directions, 1969).

108   Dante Alighieri, Epistle XIII, 5, in *Opere minori* II, 1979, 598–643.

109   Karl Popper, "Three Views Concerning Human Knowledge," in H. D. Lewis, ed., *Contemporary British Philosophy*, 3d ser. (1956), 358–388.

110   Paul A. Schlipp, ed., *Albert Einstein: Philosopher-Scientist* (Cambridge: Cambridge University Press, 1920).

111   Folder "Santayana, George," 1562, 16 Nov. 1940, BRBL. *Ezra Pound e la scienza*, 47.

112   Pound is opposing the Italian philosopher Benedetto Croce's concept of art as put forth in *Estetica* (*Problemi d'estetica* (1910); *Breviario d'estetica* (1912); *Nuovi saggi d'estetica* (1920); *Ultimi saggi* (1935); *Poesia* (1936), that is, art as expression of a moment of a pure intuition preceding the moment of philosophical knowledge. Pound opposes this idea of art as intuition because it implies that philosophical knowledge represents a higher level in the hierarchy of knowledge, from which art is excluded. However, the real meaning Croce gave to this hierarchy is controversial, and Croce himself went back to it in order to clarify it.

113   For *technê* see nn. 15 and 38 above. After Pound's reading of Aristotle's *Nicomachaean Ethics*, he focused on "constructive elements in society . . . containing the small part of intelligentia (or the real intelligentia)" and "producers . . . capable of producing." See *Guide to Kulchur*, 349.

114   In a letter to H. Rackham (1939; BRBL; Folder "H. Rackham"), Pound wrote: "The omission of *technê* from the kinds of intelligence appears to me the starting point of decadence of Western thought." For Pound's denunciation of the omission of *technê* see also n. 52 above.

115   "Have I indicated my letch towards *technê*, and do I manage to indicate what I conceive as kindred tendency. From the *thing* to the grouped things, thence to a more real knowledge. . . . The decline of the West occurred between the *Nicomachean Ethics* and *Magna* (or fat) *Moralia*." See letter to George Santayana (1940), in Paige, ed., *The Selected Letters of Ezra Pound*, 333.

116   Pound in *Guide to Kulchur* criticizes this Aristotelian hierarchy, which puts the theoretical as the highest (p. 338). In *Guide to Kulchur*, 385, Pound puts forth *technê* in terms that he will reconsider in "Pragmatic Aesthetics," that is, the Aristotelian *technê* in *Guide to Kulchur* is considered the first of the five kinds of knowing which can exist without the other kinds of knowledge ("*Therefore tending,*" 328).

117   The connection between art and history was made via Vico by Croce (see esp. *Breviario d'estetica*) and also from Gentile through various essays, although the approach of the Italians was mostly idealist.

118   Pound probably read *Magna Moralia* in the second half of the 1930s. His edition of Aristotle's *Metaphysics*, Books X–XIV (1935), also contained *Oeconomica* and *Magna Moralia*. See n. 15 above.

Machine Art

Machine Art (1927–1930)

The Plastic of Machines

This subject, "The Plastic of Machines," begins for a man the moment he stops to consider a machine as something looked at; and to ask himself whether its form is good to look at or annoying to look at, or to perceive *as form*. My second chapter, "The Acoustic of Machines," deals with the sound made by machinery, and the problems that arise from this sound.

My own conclusions are as follows:

1. The beauty of machines (A.D. 1930) is now chiefly to be found in those parts of machines where the energy is most concentrated.

2. In so far as form is concerned, the static parts of machinery obey, probably, the same aesthetics as any other architecture, and offer comparatively little field for thought *about form*.

3. Interest for the critic of form will lie mainly in the mobile parts and in the parts which more immediately hold these mobile parts in their loci.

It is here that the inventor's thought, or more probably the thought of a whole series of inventors has been most concentrated.

4. It seems possible that any man intending to practice the plastic arts; or to know excellent from mediocre or inefficient in the plastic arts might, in our time, more readily awaken his eye by looking at spare parts and at assembled machinery than by walking through galleries of painting or sculpture . . . not because a rolling press is necessarily a more pleasing spectacle than a wall painted by Cosimo Tura, but because people, as we now know them, can hardly look at anything as *form*.

They look at a portrait and wonder whether they would like to know the lady who sat, etc. . . . or whether the emotions of the painter were such as would ultimately produce a state of satisfied satiety, or titillation in themselves, etc.

Nothing is more difficult for our contemporaries than the disentanglement of their combined or even messy ideas into components.

5. And to put it another way, the plastic, or, if you insist on the use of a much abused word, the aesthetic of machines is still in a healthy state, because one can still think about the machine without dragging in the private life and personality of the inventor.

You can show a normal low-brow a spare part and get from him a rational unprejudiced answer as to whether it is a "good shape" or a silly shape, or whether it is in good proportion, or whether it looks scamped and flimsy.

Apart from people who have received special training and a few unusually intelligent humans, it is still nearly impossible to get any such straight and unbiased answer about the *shape* of a piece of sculpture or the combination of forms in a painting.

Let us at once eject people who talk about the "beauty of machinery" before they consider its shape. Or in any case let us postpone them to the historical section.

(Conclusions continued)

6. Farm machinery has been for the most part ugly; this ugliness is common to most assemblages of machinery; or to put it another way, farm machinery is usually not a machine, in the scientist's sense, it is a lot of little machines hitched together. The hitching has been done with less thought than that expended on the actually working part.

7. The beauty of the individual or "spare" parts of machinery is at present much higher than that of the "whole machine."

The "machine" is in a much better state than is the accessory architecture of machinery for the reason already indicated. Aptitude to a given end had forced or lured the inventor or inventors of line to a point nearer perfection.

Books about painting have never been of as much use as galleries, or as rooms covered with painting. Books about art are best when they are shortest. There is not a great deal to *say* or to explain. As the reader may not have a stamping mill handy, let him look at the photos. They are mostly photos of "ordinary" machines. I mean they are machines used in contemporary commerce, not museum pieces specially constructed to be looked at and put in exhibits.

Mr. Coleman Sellers 3d has provided me with the first 13 illustrations: they are mostly pieces of a "Drill Grinder." They are the best possible material for my purpose, that is to say they show the *formal* elements of the machine. Nobody is going to be distracted from contemplation of the *shape* of these objects by thinking how they affect his morals or his religion. At least one reduces the likelihood of these causes of error to the minimum humanly possible. They do not stir one to pathos by reasons extrinsic to their form.

Already the sob-sisters have attacked even this domain but it is not yet as riddled with rhetoric and sentiment as are the other domains of art. The contending ideals of Hellenist and Neo-Christian do not invade it quite so confusingly as they would the discussion of a Greek marble.

These single parts and the foci of their action have been made by thought over thought; by layer on layer of attention. The congeries in the machine is in many cases less fortunate.

When we get to the Bliss Press we have, however, something to comfort us in an age filled by political villainies and confusions. I have known several very great sculptors, and I am not sure that any one of them would be, or would have been, able to improve the shape of this press, considered simply as an object that might even stand idle in the corner of a studio filled with other fine objects.

The Confusions

People bored with the general blatancy of machine-made "progress" have or have had a dislike of machines. The association of machines with ugliness or discomfort or pandemonium is very strong.

A whole generation or three generations of sensitives have suffered from contemporary life; they desire, quite naturally, vengeance. Any man born sensitive in America between 1865 and 1895, capable of perceiving a nuance, or of perceiving Debussy's music in 1910, has suffered and has, probably, a vast thirst for vengeance. Perfect justice might appease him with the annihilation of 20% of the population and 94% of the officials.

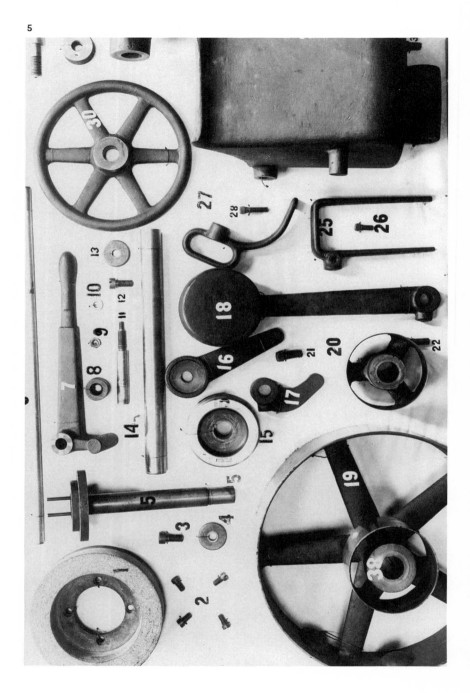

6

7

8

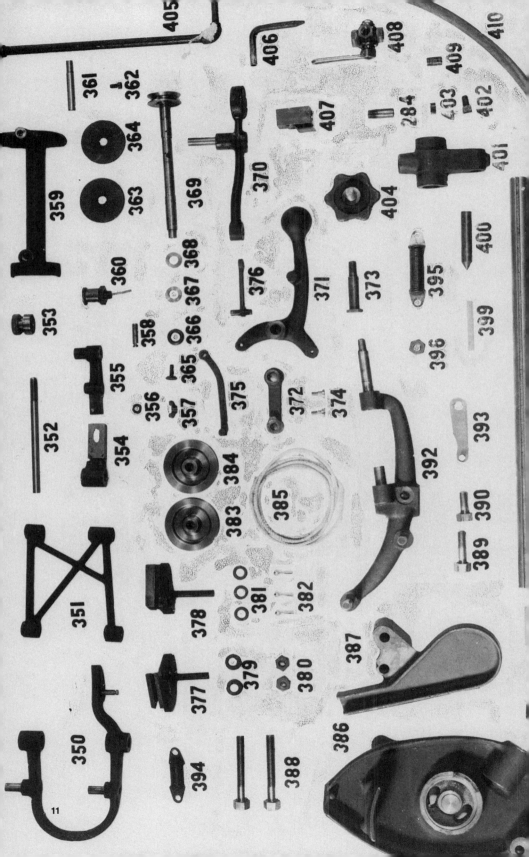

11

12

13

Mechanics, people having to do with machinery in certain ways, do not share this aversion. People who have come from the open air, and have suffered from vile working conditions are naturally fed up with machines, machinery, industry; all of which things tend to bias a judgment of machinery as form, to say nothing of the less explored field of sonority.

The Form

The necessity is to keep one's different ideas from barging into each other.

In looking at any machine one must sort out the essential parts from the parts that merely happen to be there and which keep an assemblage of machines in more or less fortuitous relation to each other.

The Bliss presses are particularly good for purpose of study because each press seems intent on its *one* particular job.

I am not so sure about the Kearsage crane. I chose it as an illustration of "Gothic" form. I dislike the Gothic, and I believe, on perhaps the too flimsy basis of hearsay, that the Kearsage crane does not work to complete satisfaction.

I suspect that cranes will be improved, and that their increasing efficiency will bring them nearer to Egyptian or Roman form. This is perhaps a wild guess, and need not be taken as an essential part of my argument.

Among the remarks about beauty that I have come upon in diverse works on philosophy, art, aesthetics, etc., I recall with pleasure the simplest: we find a thing beautiful in proportion to its aptitude to a function.

I suspect that the better a machine becomes AS A MACHINE, the better it will be to look at.

Too great care can not be taken in separating the machine itself, from its circumstance, from the fortuitous bits of metal etc., that surround it, or inside which it functions. I mean that the much vaunted Ford motor probably contains parts that give much greater *formal* satisfaction than the assembled Ford car.

When we come to automobiles deluxe, we are distracted by all sorts of related or irrelevant questions. The machine proper is hidden under its hood. All sorts of traditional aesthetics, feeling for furniture, upholstery, carosserie, enter the problem.

The best firms exhibit the chassis.

And the chassis is indubitably the more interesting phenomenon.

In its nude state it almost acquires the dignity of a work of art, it has not yet been tamed to the functions of comfort and utility. I don't want to get too lyric, but its appeal is rather more to the mind than to physical comfort.

Nevertheless, the association of known ideas is so strong that an auto chassis is far from the best example for training the eye. I mean simply that the spectator looking through the plate glass window of Rolls-Royce and Company has too many other ideas in his head to think about the shape exclusively. For that purpose he had better look at some machine whose function he does not know, and which arouses in him no expectations.

Machines and Architecture

The difference between machine plastic and the plastic of architecture is or should be perfectly clear.

The architectural work does not move; it has only its problems of stasis. Or one might put the three plastics in order: Sculpture: concerned with the form of its outside (stationary).

Architecture: concerned with the form of its outside (stationary), and *should* also be concerned somewhat with the relation of this outside to its inside.

Machinery: from the moment we consider it as having a plastic: concerned with its form in motion.

This form you may consider in relation to its aptitude to an end.

Historically, you probably do consider it as arising out of the necessity of suiting this end.

It is hardly more than parenthetical to suggest that machinery started without any consideration of its form, and solely as a utility.

There supervened a period of hideous "machine *products*," machine made ornament etc. And it is largely from a dead mental association with machine *products*, that many people still retain an idea that machines are ugly; or maintain an antipathy to machines.

Fernand Léger and several other men at one time experimented with "ideal" machines; i.e. with simply combining machine-like forms, to see whether they could improve on these shapes and shape combinations.

They mostly gave it up, and Léger, at any rate, came to the conclusion that the real machines were better *in form*, and that their actual functioning was conducive to better form.

Considering the plastic of *form in motion*, we are brought almost suddenly to our second set of perceptions. I mean from considering a space art which never ceases to be a space art, we find ourselves on the brink of considering time and recurrence.

The whole of this chapter is successful if it brings the reader to notice what I have already caused various individuals to notice, I mean as they have come into this flat, and sniffed or snorted at the idea of my writing a book about machines or illustrating a review with photographs of machinery.

What one can see from the photos is simply that they record forms that are *interesting* in themselves, and in their combinations.

That I in particular should notice this, causes me no surprise, nor can I see in it any incongruity. The perception of a statue by Gaudier or Brancusi, or the perception of a stamping press has never so far as I know dimmed my perception of a statue by Mino da Fiesole or of a painting by Piero della Francesca, or, for that matter, of a rhythm in one of Arnaut's canzoni.

J. B. Alberti who made the first designs for the Temple of Rimini wrote a treatise on painting in which he says: "The architect gets his idea from the painter."

This saying has become almost incomprehensible with the passage of centuries. One needs a head full of Giotto and Cimabue, and various other impressions, to understand what Alberti was driving at.

It seems to me quite possible that some modern dilettante or empiric architect might as well write: the architect gets his idea from the machine shop.

A little clarity here, might save one a good deal of vague talk about, and vague misunderstanding of, Zeitgeists.

The best modern architects are, I suppose, almost universally the engineers; their best form comes from the mathematics of strains, etc. rather than from any thought about pictorial qualities. Their worst effects come from their trimmings. But the best engineers are possibly in our time the engineers of machinery. All this is an aside, a general speculation. But . . . our buildings are inferior to our machinery. And the architect's best lesson may very possibly lie in the machine.

With our perception of motion we are led to that sonority, that is, to the measure and computation of sonorities in acoustic.

The Acoustic of Machinery

"The ear is an organ for the detection of frequency."
"Music is a composition of frequencies."
—E.P. in *Treatise on Harmony*

The reader may start either with my brochure on Antheil or with that charming cartoon, "El Rivetor," which greeted Mr. Antheil's performance in New York (April 1927).

The cartoon was both wrong and right. Mr. Johnstone's suggestion that the asphalt drill was "flat" is irresistibly (from Mr. Johnstone's point of view) funny.

Nobody has yet heard a New York street corner plus excavation plus steel construction conglomerate, harmonized, and so far as I can perceive, no one will. Construction work is done only once and without rehearsal. Factory work is done day after day, and people can and do practice the best way of doing it. The idea that a factory, or at least the more highly organized and organizable parts of a factory can not be "harmonized" is no sillier in 1927, than the idea that a horseless carriage could move, was in, let us say, 1880. The only reason the engineers have not done it already is because no one had thought of it.

To think of it, and to think of it as possible, one had to be, perhaps, sensitive. One had to like and to dislike sound, I mean to like some kinds and arrangements of sound, and to dislike others. One had to be of those for whom *"le monde sonore existe,"* those for whom the "world of sonority" has an existence.

And one had to think of music as a definite entity in itself; that is to say, as a composition of sound; not merely an *expression of* something else, let us say the *expression of* a nightingale, or of a melancholy young man with a belly-ache.

There is nothing against considering music as the *expression of* x, y, z, grandeur, the Shakespearean megalaciousness of Beethoven, etc. I mean there is nothing against it, except that it may prevent a man's ever coming up against the hard fact, or understanding what music is made out of. To understand the not-clay, not-stone, not-bronze that the musician *uses* to express himself.

"I made it, out of a mouthful of air," Yeats boasts of a poem in *The Wind Among the Reeds*.

I made it deciding *when* a man should scrape cat gut, and how long, and how taut the piece of cat gut should be when he scrapes it.

The miracle of a Bach sonata is in the knowledge, and the justness of his decision.

The dignity of music obviously does not lie in the "material sonore"; it is not in the bull's hide, or the cat-gut, or the composed brass of the Sarussophone.

I tried to point out in my brochure on Antheil that harmony as studied, the history of the scale, etc., had hitherto dealt with frequencies from 8 or 16 to the second, up to 36,000 per second; but that lower frequencies than these had always been used in music, and that no musician could escape using them, and that the more intelligently he used them, the better his music would be. Hence, historically, jazz.

Masterly rhythm is but savant demarcation of frequency. Masterly harmonic progression is but savant demarcation of frequencies.

Obviously a boiler factory will never sound like a nocturne of Chopin, but to say that the sound in a boiler factory can never receive a savant demarcation is as foolish as it would be for a cutter of cameos to say that no building could ever be beautiful because buildings are much too big.

To say that there are many obstacles, to say that it requires infinite time and patience, to say that it may not pay (at once), is merely to face a few things that the least poet or artist has always faced without any great repugnance, since the beginnings of recorded emotion.

No noise in a factory has ever shocked me as much as the bells in Old North Church, which started to chime while I was near them in the Belfry. No sound as utterly hideous as the chimes of Kensington Church, London has ever struck on my tympanum, to say nothing of the inanity, the blatant and disgusting malevolence that causes this biweekly noise.

When I consider the disagreeable noises I have heard in factories it seems to me that they are mainly disagreeable for one sole reason, namely they are not organized. Some screech continues too long; some repeat is irregular in an unpleasant manner.

Part of this *may* be due to "the needs of the work." The needs of the "work" constitute part of the technical problem. Other noises are not inherent in the needs of the work, they are merely noises that have not been considered as sonority. No one has thought of utilizing them for the ease and refreshment of the workers. They are waste and bad practice. Just as bad ventilation is bad policy.

If you are an artist "for whom the sonorous world exists," this thing is a problem; just as interesting as, let us say a problem of foreshortening was to Holbein or Mantegna.

The difficulty, the magnitude of the sounds, the need of using "great bass," does not detract from the problem.

Note: The term *bass* is used in music to designate the lesser frequencies (low notes), the term *treble*, to designate the higher frequencies. I use the term *"great bass"* to designate the frequencies below those which the ear has been accustomed to consider as "notes."

The asphalt drill may not be, in the current sense "flat," but it may very well be in the current sense, "slow."

Napoleon thought Fulton a charlatan.

The main difficulty for the layman is that he is used to thinking of the beauty of music as something which happens during the tenth of a second—the "sweetness" of Campanini's high C, the bulbul note of Madame Kazumm the soprano, etc.

You are not going to get this sweetness out of a stamping press, any more than you are going to find building surface polished like the face of a sapphire.

In composing NOISE, you will have, to some extent, to neglect what the music schools now call pitch, but this really means that you will neglect or struggle against a known and explored set of high pitches, and make your composition in much lower pitch.

Instead of a key of C major, you will start with a related "great bass" key, you will take, say, 256 to the minute instead of to the second as your "tonic."

Mathematically it is just as easy to work out a scale, tonic, second, third, sub-dominant, dominant, sixth, seventh, octave, for the frequency per minute, as it is to work out such a scale in frequencies per second.

Puristically, one might have the fun of starting fresh without the mess of the tempered piano.

Practically one will be lucky if one gets as far in the 20th Century with "great bass" as, let us say, the 11th Century got with melody. Young?

This art is not yet past the midwife. A definite result demands, like any other definite result in the arts, the genius.

Nothing proves that a simple transposition of "Ein Feste Burg" into great bass is going to prove a felicitous action.

There is still less to prove that Bliss and Company or Coleman Sellers could use it.

It seems to me that the thing will start with some crank fooling about his machine shop after hours; or some foreman stopping a few presses for three seconds, every eight minutes; or by some equally simple experiment . . . some experiment that will put a rhythm into the work.

One effect that I have particularly noticed in the U.S. Mint, occurs when some "unbearable noise" rip'rip'rip' is reinforced by another still louder and apparently faster BRIPRIPBIPBIBBIBBP!!

Nearly all kids LIKE noise. It is very hard to get them to pipe down. No one has yet made a study of the effect of female neurasthenic headaches on the "Ideal of the Beautiful in Music."

It is very difficult to persuade a healthy male child that the melancholy piping of the piano is pleasant.

I don't want to boost my private and personal sensibility, but it seems to me that one's *first* interest in sound comes either from very loud or very delicate sounds.

This seems to me perfectly natural, as the middling loud sounds, in middling pitch, strike on parts of the ear already full of association with ordinary things, things from which one's interest has been exhausted.

I don't mean that the best music may not be made, and probably has been and is made in the middle of the register. I am talking of the awakening of interest. This usually starts from an unusual perception or stimulus.

Lemmi Rossi with his "sistema," and ten dozen other Renaissance theorists, all worked at "proportions" and other now dead details, then necessary to musical theory. Machine acoustic will not be charted and elaborated in a week or ten days.

Machine plastic is already equal to other plastic. The object exists; the man in the shop may or may not be able to see it, or he may have too many associations with it to judge it clearly.

One eminent man of letters argues that he *has* associated ideas regarding any piece of machinery. I don't much believe it. At any rate he must have fewer associations with the spare part of some machine whose function is unknown to him, than with machines which have; and so even for his sophisticated and possibly beclouded mind, the machine part offers a chance of perceiving form unaffected.

But between the plastic and acoustic of machinery there is the greatest possible gap; the gap between a thing done, a thing in a high state of development and the thing not yet, or scarce yet, attempted.

Note on Antheil

The subject being new, the misconceptions are likely to outnumber the perceptions. Nothing could be further from my desire than to take impressions of noise. The Futurists went in for impressions of noise, machine noise, probably à la Schumann. It is not for me a question of taking an impression of machine noise and reproducing it in the concert hall or of making any more noise, but composing, governing the noise that we've got.

And the "idea" comes to me, or came in part from Antheil (who did not for the moment develop it) and in part from two compositions by Antheil, his First violin sonata, and his Ballet Mécanique as played by him first on one Pleyela, and, later on ONE Pleyela, with bells, buzzers, and amplifier.

The genesis of the "Ballet Méchanique," especially the part finally *rejected* goes back at least to 1916, at which time Alvin Coburn and I invented the vortoscope. In 1920 or 21 Dudley Murphy applied this simple device to cinematography. We took a few metres of interesting and highly unsatisfactory film. Man Ray with his brilliant record and long experience produced something infinitely better; Murphy combined with Léger and got some interesting results.

The boredom both for the homme de lettres and the musician was past all bearing. Antheil's ballet outgrew its original setting.

It will be seen by this that Mr. Wyndham Lewis is right, I am an individual so lacking in personal character, principles, etc., that I am ready to take up with Arnaut Daniel, Arnold Dolmetsch, Propertius, or any photographer in search of abstract design, or a modus of presenting forms moving. And moreover, I remain unrepentant.

It is doubtless a marvelous and sinister coincidence that having played in the elevator like other American infants, and having at the age of four and from thence onward been taken often through the press rooms of the Mint and seen all that active brightness of presses, fires and crucibles, I should meet later, talk to, and even waste time with a few young Americans who had also looked at machinery, or taken an interest in form.

You can no more take machines out of the modern mind, than you can take the shield of Achilles out of the *Iliad*.

Of all machinery, war machinery is the least interesting and had possibly the longest and fullest tradition. They had war machines in Byzantium so solid that they were found in working order three hundred years after the date of construction. They had also a pestilent bureaucracy. One could do without either. One will probably have to do without them if one wants, as a nation, to leave a more interesting record than that of Byzantium.

Sociology of Machines

I leave this section to Charles W. Wood. It is possible that machinery will lead men to cooperate more sanely, and break up a too virulent concept of private property, in so far as that concept relates to machines; or it is equally possible that it won't, and that a nation imbecile enough to produce our current bureaucracy, copyright villainy, customs cretinism and paraphernalia, will merely fall into the pit of Byzantinism.

The aim of economy, according to the more enlightened economists is to release more energy for invention and design. Bureaucracy doesn't.

Machines do not move against the amenities. The engineering mind is about the most satisfactory mind of our time; like all other mind types, it has its borders, but the practice of engineering seems to me less stultifying than most other contemporary practices. It does not seem to me, and I do not see how it can be, built up by layer after layer of bunk.

For example, when the engineering mind tackles the problem of the utter uselessness of many alleged government officials, the utter needless obscurantism and obstructionism of their "functions," it seems to me that the engineering mind will clear away a good deal of this superstition. It will experiment. It will come clear-headedly to perceptions unclogged by fixed ideas.

It will, or should, appear to the engineer that it is inefficient to employ people to do for one, and more especially to interfere with one's doing, things that one can perfectly well do for oneself.

It seems to me that the engineering mind, even a little released from immediate problems, or given that much extra leisure for "invention and design" might lead to a sort, and a very sane sort of Confucianism; non-interference and order.

When this happens, a lot of public nuisances, passport officials, customs officials, in fact about 85% of all "functionaries" will be sent to the scrap. I don't mean they will of necessity be killed off or starved. But it will be found to be cheaper, more expeditious, more efficient, to pay them to live in complete idleness than to allow them to interfere in any way with the active and productive private members of the community.

Nothing could be more entertaining (at least personally entertaining to the present author) than the way in which flap-doodle professorial economics have given way to engineers' economics.

To the engineering mind, a state will probably appear decadent in just the degree that there *are* numbers of inhibitory or uselessly tabulative persons employed to interfere with, and inquire into the actions of others.

The tyrant is biologically preferable to the bureaucrat, at least he has in him some principle of life and of action. The bureaucracy is mere rust and fungus, all the more dangerous because of the imperceptible pace of its ravages.

Objections to Machines

Objection to machines has probably disappeared from all, save a few belated crania. No machine ever interfered with a man's personality or damaged his liberty. Machines were made to eliminate work and produce leisure. Overcrowding, bad placing, bad ventilation of work rooms, all these results of greed and ineradicable human stupidity may have done harm, but can not be blamed on the machine. Machine products have been ugly but even the parochial aesthetic knows by now that this is due to human stupidity and not to machines; the same result has occurred in handwork, painting, music, whenever the worker or artist has gone in for flummydiddle instead of proportion.

Faith

Modern man can live and should live in his cities and machine shops with the same kind of swing and exuberance that the savage is supposed to have in his forest. —E.P. in *Workshop Orchestration*

That might almost be my last word on the subject.

And Yet . . .

As one never gets any statement too clear, I may as well stress a few points, even if I bore the more perspicuous reader with repetition. The point of the Antheil ballet is *not* that it makes "the one hell of a row." The Antheil ballet as circus, the Antheil ballet as source of literary impressions, etc. . . . is all very well for the dilettante. If the fat lady in the box in front of one is jumping up and down on her seat saying: "It's so exciting, it's so ecitingitz, so ecciting, it's . . ." and the rest is lost in a storm of jeers, cheers, etc. . . . in short if a man has speculated on his ticket, and if he enjoys the hurly-burly of excited crowd, etc., that is "one pair of sleeves," but I can not be expected to consider these things an integral part of the composition which I heard first in the composer's apartment and later at rehearsal in the empty Theatre Champs Elysée.

For me the impressions of the pleyela role of the ballet are mainly two, first that it makes a great deal of noise in certain places, secondly that the main effect is *restful*, namely all this clatter and clangor is brought into order, is put under some sort of control, and after the first shock or exacerbation there succeeds a feeling of calm, and of, if you like, the mind or will of the composer producing this order. I am inclined to think that this effect increases as one becomes more familiar with the composition. As for Antheil's musical competence and sense of métier, one need only examine the early contrapuntal work, four of the short pieces for piano, called for some reason six "sonatas," and the first and third sonatas for violin and piano.

Both as a step in the history of music, and as the transition point from concert music into machine-composition, the ballet is important. Musically, the point is that Antheil uses the longer durations; the divisions of time are so big that the NOISE is, as it were, swallowed up by them, or at any rate brought into proportion with something else of corresponding magnitude. It is perhaps not quite just to graph it:

duration : loudness.
There is some sort of triple relation:
duration : silence : loudness.

When I say that composition for machines will have a key in "great
bass," I naturally do not mean that what is now called "pitch" will be
eliminated, any more than time is eliminated by Mozart when he com-
poses in E flat. I merely think that as a practical start the organizing will
have to begin with the great bass and that the various kinds of noise,
compounds of pitches and overtones will be fitted into it.

Sociology

The sociology of the question does not belong to this book, it impinges
a little, possibly, because Charles W. Wood is one of the few intelligent
men now writing in America and thinking at all about the effects of machinery.

He sees big plants leading, if not to communism, at least to some sort
of combination-thinking or group thinking, etc. We had something of
this sort from Jules Romains years ago with his Unanimisme, though he
was not thinking about machines in 1910.

One may as well look at other possibilities and likelihoods. The state,
if we could but rid our minds of superficial appearance, is probably, now
in our time, simply the banking business. This is not new, the Medici
state was simply the banking business, banking business with hardly
any trimmings or camouflage. It succeeded a sort of democracy.

An organization like Henry Ford's is probably feudal. I use the word
here with a sense of, relatively, very high commendation; it implies the
responsibility of the overlord to his vassals; and implies a very different
mode of thought from that implied in the abusive term "industrial system" or "industrialism." To put it another way, I might say that Kublai
Khan's power was founded on finance and pillage, the Byzantine empire
was founded on money (backed by war machinery and bureaucracy),
feudalism was founded on produce, or on produce plus service, obliga-
tions, and a good deal of sentiment. If you don't like this last term, call
it "good will."

The people who have sneered at Ford's biography in my presence
have been people who have not read it.

The conflicts between the old modalities of thought change very slowly, I don't know that they change at all fundamentally, there is an infinite change on the surface.

The cathedral of Modena is said to have been built by mass action, but the passage that makes this claim for it is very brief, and does not go into any elucidative detail.

All speculations about the ultimate social effects of machinery are really outside the scope of this brochure.

As for Ford himself, I see no reason to disguise my interest in either his theories or his practice. *He has already experimented in tempo.*

He might have a dozen reasons for not experimenting in sonority. There might be any number of obstacles; there might be any number of reasons, invisible in Rapallo, why experiments or the practice of sonorous division would not give an immediate yield in the auto or tractor business; but I should be very much surprised if Ford found the idea utterly mad, or its ultimate practice unthinkable.

Naturally the only people I want to talk to about it are shop-engineers; the theory of musical proportions is already written down in books and easily available.

As I have said elsewhere, there is no reason why the shop noise shouldn't be used as stimulus and to give swing and ease to modern work, just as the sailor's chantey or any working song has been used, by lumbermen, or by savages.

I don't know how to make it simpler even for people totally ignorant of musical theory. The proportions of the major scale are:

	1	9/8	5/4	4/3	3/2	5/3	15/8	2
or	do	re	mi	fa	so	la	si	do
	24	27	30	32	36	40	45	48

There are slightly different relations in minor scales; but all music is built out of fundamentally simple combinations of frequency. That is to say the vibrations of two notes meet, separate, meet, separate, you start with two notes that do this fairly often, say once every third, fourth, or fifth vibration. This becomes too obvious and you add a third note to the chord, meeting now the first note, now the second note; and all three of them meeting once say in 30 times.

A sheer speculation I should think one would have to take a very slow recurrence for machines, I mean slow in comparison with the vibration of a fiddle string; and I *think* the screeching pitch of many factory noises would have to be neglected in one's first efforts, more or less as overtones are neglected in most musical computation.

The harmonization would consist (1) in bringing the different percussive speeds of the machinery into some regular proportion, where possible; (2) in establishing some proportion between the uninterrupted duration of the noises.

As I said in a former note on *Workshops*, I *think* that even very short silences can be used with great effect; I mean silences that would have no appreciable effect on the work. Simply the duration of the silence must have a definite proportion to the noise, i.e. be in tune.

There will be many analogies with the very simple facts about music that should be found at the beginning of any book on harmony.

My addition, if it is an addition, is simply to insist that the recurrences below those which the ear recognizes as sound, can be brought into relation with each other; and that a use of these recurrences in proportion to each other will have some effect on human nerves; and that it can be combined with "higher" recurrences known as notes, and that the resultant disturbance of the atmosphere may even "give pleasure" or at any rate be less nerve racking and wearing than wholly unorganized clatter.

The musical ethnologist will here interpose, "Addition, fiddlesticks! The Japanese and the Africans have been using these 'lower recurrences' for the past thirty-four hundred years. What's the use dragging in technical terms?"

Very well. The shop engineer has a more complicated orchestra at his disposal; he has the chance of dealing with something more complicated than the tom-tom, or that of the *in* and *yo* of the Japanese singing, and accompaniment of drums in the Noh, with basic proportion of 5 and 7.

(At this point a charming lady of the olde school rises to say that I am "jealous of music.") To proceed: the next step will probably be made, if it is made, by someone who knows his shops, and who *listens*.

The solutions for one kind of shop will not be applicable to another, although they might be suggestive of further solutions. A great deal of electric machinery makes no noise whatever, or merely a gently somniferous purr.

When it comes to this listening, Antheil's music may be useful. Antheil at the age of 26 has not revealed all music or all possible music "of the future." I suggest, simply that from two of his works the serious auditive might get hints; he might find in them clues to a way of dealing with machinery, and bringing its noise under control. These compositions are a start, not a finish.

As to the plastic, a man can not learn plastic by reading books, he can only learn it by looking at objects. All the "critic" can do for him is to knock him out of his habitual associations, to "show him the thing in a new light" or better, put it somewhere he hadn't expected to find it.

How to Write

How to Write (1930)

Leaving the question of melopoeia a list of rules of thumb that I tabulated 18 years ago are still as useful as anything available to me in an endeavour to help the reader. I was not composing a complete Art of Poesy. I was trying to avoid discussion of what constitutes good poetry by using a less general title. I called it Imagism. The term has since been debased. I laid down three main propositions.

I. Direct treatment of the thing whether objective or subjective.
II. To use no word that does not contribute to the presentation.
III. To compose in the sequence of the melodic phrase and in the sequence of the metronome.

I next composed a list of Don'ts intended to supplement the rejection slip of a certain magazine. These Don'ts were aimed at the current faults of poetry in 1912. Certain modifications in styles of error have since taken place but the list needs no deletions. Either I or the reader can supply the omissions.

This list has definitely functioned for nearly twenty years. I offer it without apology. It has had a pragmatic or de facto sanction. On the other hand a great many writers have tried to go round behind it, innumerable writers have sunk into desuetude or failed to rise out of it by trying to avoid the second main proposition.

Since 1912 Mr. Eliot has arisen. In Mr. Eliot's wake has appeared the new Gongorism which I mentioned in my note on Dunning in *Exile*, 3, 1928 before Professor X had written a book on the subject. That supplies perhaps the main fault omitted from my early list.

The danger even among the cleverest of the new Gongorists is that the attention paid to the individual word is so great that it detracts from the main sense of the poem.

In Góngora the detail was trope or ornament or floridity (a "beauty" or an ornament). In the post-Cummingsites and even in Cummings when he is not at his best, the cleverness of the single word or phrase, or the close crop of a dozen assorted clever cuts distracts from the main subject or even excludes a main subject.

There are probably only a certain number of main literary diseases. They crop up in different places and eras with superficial alteration.

Sincere means without wax, sine cera, but there is nothing on its surface to tell us that Roman antique dealers and makers of fake expensive marble used wax for their frauds. They still use it for that purpose in Naples.

However, the King with his dog on a beat, or the king with a soldier; meaning the one to amble or picnic and the other a military expedition hold their due content for the eye and the wit.

The elder sister, the moving eye.

The elder brother, the moving mouth, have their satire.

The ideograph is a door into a different modality of thought. I do not believe that one can save the reader much time or the printer much space by trying to open this door in fewer words than Professor Fenollosa has used. And I therefore give the essay as an appendix.

There are two points I would make here:

1) that good poetry in European languages often seems to fit into ideograph. *The Seafarer* for example.

When we come to examine this statement more closely we see the ideograph as it were absorbs our phanopoeia or our good imagism and then makes place for another quality. It takes the static image. You might almost say that it is the static image before one attempts to write. But if you try to put the static image into ideograph you at once feel the void. The ideograph wants the moving image, the concrete thing plus its action.

The further he goes the less he knows about the subject of his discourse.

On the other hand, the ideograph abstracts or generalizes in the known concrete. For example the picture letter for red is composed of the four signs meaning respectively:

Rose, cherry, iron-rust and flamingo.

Whatever the inconveniences of this form of writing it has for poetry a great value. It is a treasure house of concrete images.

The thing is what it does. "The true noun as isolated thing does not exist in nature. Things are only the terminal points or rather the meeting points of actions, cross sections, snapshots. The eye sees noun and verb in one, things in action, action in things and so the Chinese conception tends to represent them."

"The sun underlying the bursting forth of plants = spring. The sun tangled in the branches of the tree sign = east. Rice field plus struggle = male."

In character after character one finds these solid ideas. Poetic or humorous, full of pith as a peasant's hard observation. Carrying down in picture open to anyone who knows the signs what only a few of our words carry for the trained philologist.

I mean to say that we have known the history of our words before we can extract the long held flavour.

Somewhere in the earlier part of this booklet I said that we must try to see in what different ways the language had been charged with meaning. The word as eye-memory is obviously a very different battery from the word as ear-memory.

Apart from studying these two different but by no means mutually hostile systems I know of only one other.

The more one reflects, meditates on the capacity of the Chinese system the more one sees its advantages for phanopoeia. I don't think they are either depressing or discouraging.

Printed with a proper crib a Chinese poem is as clear to us as it is to the Jap who reads it with a gloss in Japanese script.

I see no reason why the Chinese classics should not be printed for us in this manner. Mori and Ariga wrote out some two hundred poems in this manner for Fenollosa.

Another stimulus came from Africa; it is not so important for our purpose but it is not negligible. Lévy-Bruhl points out the savage's lack of power to generalize. He has forty verbs where we have two or three verbs and some adverbs. The savage language grades down into pantomime and mimicry.

What Lévy-Bruhl says about the verbs of savages, what Fenollosa says about verbs in Chinese, what I had written about Dante's verbs before I had heard of Fenollosa all joins up. The good writer need not throw over anything humanity has acquired but he will in the measure of his genius try to recover the vividness of Dante, Li Po and the bushman. The savage to whom the wood or the bend in the river is not a wood or a bend but one particular stretch of wood, one particular bend in that river.

Sneers at "mouldy reminiscences of Pan" do not cover the matter.

Further Exposition

When I had succeeded in "placing" a rougher version of the foregoing program three publishers desired to print my collected prose. It was then discovered that I had written half of a million words in my attempt to arrive at my conclusions. It was also intimated that there was no practical way of printing and marketing half a million words on this subject. There was also a crisis in the American book trade. This crisis as I see it was and is at the moment I write this (July 22, 1930) due to a fear that the American public is too stupid to buy books without buying bindings. The continental European buys books in paper covers at 50 or 60 cents per volume in order to see what is in them very much as the American buys magazines. The cry that cheaper books means standardization and "Fordizing" is sheer hypocrisy or incomprehension of what Ford has done with the automobile. The crass American publisher did not try to Fordize. Ford sold cheap automobiles that would run and that were supposed to last a certain time. The book trade overproduced books that would not run, i.e. they were inferior junk, they were novels, etc., that were forgotten in five years or less, or the works of "great authors" that lasted ten years and couldn't last longer. There was no attempt to achieve literary efficiency. The system demanded vast "overhead," literature was expected to carry huge staffs of clerks and pay for expensive offices. As usual the printer was put above the author.

Phanopoeia

Whether Ernest Fenollosa ever used his essay on the Chinese Written Character as a lecture at any time before his death in 1908 I do not know. I think it probable that he may have done so. In 1919 after three years effort that very considerably lowered my opinion of editorial intelligence I succeeded in getting this study into print. The lack of attention given it after it was in print (first in the *Little Review* and then in *Instigations*) has gone far to increase my contempt for the intelligence of the general reader and for a number of distinguished literati whom I had until that date more or less "believed in."

The main disassociation in this essay is between the Chinese and occidental modes of thought. Fenollosa attacks logic in favour of science. The logic appears to him occidental and the scientific approach to knowledge appears to him to be also the poetic and to be the way inherent in the Chinese ideograph as distinct from occidental phonetic writing.

His concrete instance is that if you ask an European: "What is red?" he will say "Red is a colour."

What is colour? Colour is a refraction of light. What is light? Light is a vibration.

What is vibration? Vibration is a form of energy.

What is energy? Energy is a mode of being.

What is being? etc.

That is to say, the European mind moves from the concrete known to the general and to the still more general unknown.

The overlord and advertiser was set above both.

I leave this paragraph in order that this booklet may serve as a record as well as a manual.

Nevertheless, the following summary must be understood in relation to the uncollected half million words of exposition, just as the sentence in a law case must be understood more or less in relation to the court proceedings which have previously taken place.

If my collected notes are ever printed even they will be found to be in apparent disproportion, i.e., some topics treated very fully and some apparently passed over without due attention. That is because certain points seem to me to have been more or less "settled" or at least to stand in less need of discussion. You do not ask a researching chemist to present a solution of all formulae. You expect him to know what has been done before he starts and to relate his work to existing "science," and to rectify it where possible. In literary history and criticism certain things appeared to me in need of rectification. The half million words is an attempt at such rectification and neither an encyclopedia nor a complete and universal history of letters.

In all but the largest histories of English literature the works of the great translators are slighted. In all the histories of this literature that I have seen, the functioning of translation in the development of the art of writing English is completely neglected.

Plenty of professorial persons note that Shakespeare found his plots in such and such "sources," but that is a totally different matter. The comparison of the quality of the writing in Chaucer as translator and Chaucer as original author is not, so far as I know, even hinted at. The comparison of Gavin Douglas and Golding to precedent and later poets is not made.

I don't know that the critics have even discussed or even tried to understand how the study of a foreign classic can stimulate and foster the art of writing.

Melopoeia

Neither do I know quite how I am to illustrate the value of Greek verse for people who do not know enough Greek even to understand the sound of particular quotations. Perhaps they will have to take it on faith and on the witness of historic example. Simply: it has been found that the study of Greek verse rhythms does ameliorate the verse rhythms of the particularly and peculiarly gifted student.

Somewhere about 1440 Bassinio argued in Rimini that a study of Greek was necessary to the pleasant writing of good Latin. You can still see scraps of Greek in the margins of his manuscripts, Greek cadences that he had used as pace makers for his narrative of the siege of Vada. And Bassinio in the *Isoteus* probably wrote a good share of the real poetry that was composed in the Latin of the Renaissance. Swinburne's revitalization of English rhythm was hatched of his Greek. In his manuscript there was presumably a vast memory, a capacity for reciting scenes at a time.

I am not sure that people understand even here how the mechanism works or wrecks to best advantage. There is in biology the classic story of Agassiz, the student and the quite common fish. The student recognized the common fish, he described it in a few pages. Agassiz did not change the fish; he sent the student back to dissect it and to "look at it."

Von Sternberg gave Antheil a fugue theme. He had him write a fugue every week for a year NOT on a new theme each week but on the same theme for the whole year.

It is not the quantity of matter that passes under the eye of the observer but the intensity of the observation that counts.

Were I to make a small anthology on the principles exposed in my program, I should be disquietingly aware of a danger: the danger of creating a new academicism. If that program were taken as the program of the old curricula has been taken for so long, this danger would be very real. It is not expedient that the student should accept my opinion about any given passage.

After the Greek melopoeia came the Provençal. I am glad that I found the latter first. I perfectly well understand that if the student starts with Greek he has great difficulty in climbing from the Greek point of view to a point of view based on comparison of a dozen tongues.

On the other hand, if a promising metrist came to me in this year (1930) and asked for instruction in let us say things that I myself do not know, I might very possibly tell him to read ten lines of the *Odyssey* daily. I don't know whether I read the *Odyssey* as the Homeric Greeks read it. For the purpose of enjoying its rhythm, it does not matter one tittle whether one reads it with philologic correctness; what matters is getting from it a fecund and exciting rhythmic sensation. This can be done if one reads it with the following beliefs: 1) musicality of verse depends on a use of constants and variants;
2) in the case of Greek hexameter rhythm the quantity is supposedly the constant and the position of the accent, the variant. As a matter of fact the quantity is a variable within limits very much greater than permitted in English "pentameter" (accentual).

Whether or not any Greek professor would approve of my reading of Greek, it is impossible for me to read a page anywhere in the *Odyssey* without discovering something rhythmically interesting, often "new" (i.e. to me) and stimulating.

I doubt if it is possible for anyone to say anything new about the literary validity of the poem, and shall not attempt to do so.

The sapphic strophe is so beautiful that even in very gross imitation it preserves a very great beauty. So far as I know Catullus is the only man who has ever managed to rival the original or to "get inside the mechanism." I do not believe in Horace's sapphics. There are a few English approximations; or I might say that the attempt to use the sapphic skeleton has produced a very small number of beautiful poems whose movement is very different from the *Poikilótron Phaínetaí Moi Kénos Isos Téoisin.*

I shall put short Greek citations in Latin type because the general reader does not get any impression from a line of Greek.

I think the sapphic rhythm is biological and organic, I think it is due to the structure of the female body and for that reason the male finds it very difficult to use. I think it is the direct opposite of the iambic.

Pindar appears to me to be too rhetorical to serve as a good subject of study. With the exception of the second Idyll Theocritus seems to me to belong almost to belles lettres rather than to the strong and main line of poesy.

The justification or the historical background of vers libre (Anglo-American as distinct from the break-up of the French Alexandrine) seems to me to have been very clearly presented by those editors who have given Euripides' choruses with a metric analysis, i.e., long, short, trochee, spondee, etc., carefully marked and often different in each line of a passage.

The further development of Greek rhythm, or jazz or the "introduction" of the Syrian (Arabic) element seems to be very clear in Bion's *Death of Adonis.*

I think that summarizes my reasons for presenting my list of Greek prosodists. [I have] given samples [of the] best English translators of [these] authors in my "Translators of Greek" in *Instigations.* I can't see how I can abbreviate that essay or make it [fit the] present volume.

I don't know any short cut to this source of rhythmic knowledge save that of learning enough Greek to get an idea of the movement of this poetry in the original.

The case of Provençal is simpler. Given a graph of the stropic structure and a little patience one can understand what Arnaut Daniel was melodically driving at. I shall quote my essay on Arnaut at some length because there are only two editions of him available. Any reader can get the Greek texts from any college library. The development of strophic structure continues through Provençe and into Tuscany. I have given some details in the introduction to my Cavalcanti. Roughly speaking the emphasis shifts from the sound to the meaning, and from the strophe to the individual line. Later French and English strophes are mainly simplification of the Provinçal data. They are much less interesting as strophes, and I believe that they are rhythmically less interesting as single lines and short passages than is the verse of Guido and Dante.

Con quello imaginar che mi conquise.

Io vidi donne con la donna mia
Non che niuna mi sembrasse donna
Ma simigliavan sol la sua ombria

Not only for rhythm but for the pith of meaning in both Guido and Dante, but that takes me out of the particular part of the subject I am here discussing.

The fragments of Anglo-Saxon that we have left give us the other system in which the constant is the required alliteration (repetition of the same consonant a given number of times in the line) Hlude waeron hy la hlude / Tha hy ofer thon lond rydon / Waeron anmode, tha hy ofer thon lond rydon.

We are here on another known language, I am not insisting on the reader learning a great deal of it but he must either hear it read or learn enough to guess what it sounded like, or can be made to sound like.

This brings us to the question of actual song. I do not believe one can make this subject vivid by general statement, and that is all the excuse I propose to give for autobiography and definite anecdote from life. I have tested my sense of rhythm and compared it with that of good musicians, Sir Thomas Beecham, Landowska's playing of Bach, Antheil as he was when he wrote the *Ballet Mécanique* or when he spent two months struggling with me over the proper graphs of my musical setting of Villon.

A list of the songs worth hearing or the song books worth buying looks like a jumble of odds and ends picked without system. Necessarily. The same sort of discrepancies may exist in science; certainly they exist in medicine. There are sets that are known and tracts that are unknown. There are things done and things not yet done or known or "available."

When it comes to our knowledge of the union of *motz el son*, word and tune, we are not superlatively rich in models. We have a dozen or so Provençal tunes with words, two collections (Rummel's and Bedford's) both of which I have had a hand in.

We have a few old English song books discussed by Mr. Dolmetsch. We have collections of French folk song and "everybody" objects to everybody's settings save their own. The melodies in Tierset or in Yvette's collections can be sung by a good diseur or diseuse like Tinayre or the superlative Yvette. The diseuse or diseur takes the written graph as a basis and varies the time tempo etc. of each strophe stanza.

En passant par la Loraine; Le Roi, Renaud; Le Duc de Maine or *Le Pauvre Laboureur.* The Russian songs of Moussorgsky, and so forth. I was showing the French songs and some bel canto to Roland Hayes. He was rather like a small boy in the presence of a teacher. We had not known each other very, very long. In the *Bel Canto* the words have given way to the notes. *Le Pauvre Laboureur* moved him as it should. I then got out the Kennedy Fraser Hebridean collection. The small boy and pupil suddenly vanished. A man and a brother was hammering me on the back: "Now you HAVE showed me something!!"

Here indeed we have melody and rhythm that was far enough removed geographically to escape the blight of Christian propriety and that touches the rest of the margin, the steppes and the African continent.

There is a man in Berlin named Hornbostel. He does not give public performances; he attends to the African Kultur for the German government. He has a pitch sense so exact that he does not write his melodies on the stave simply but with the pitch marked at its vibration number per second.

Our state of awareness in these matters and our state of knowledge can not remain static.

A man's context is all that he has written on a subject and on subjects allied thereto; or perhaps all he has written minus what he has corrected and erased.

One's judgements or selections of significant work are obviously due to what one sets down on paper and to a great deal that one does not set down, either because one hasn't reduced it to formulae or because one thinks that the value of an extra statement is outweighed by its tendency to distract the reader from something more important.

14

15

16

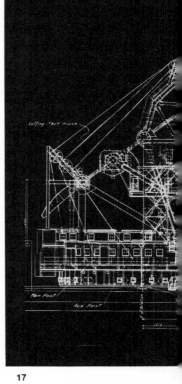

17

18

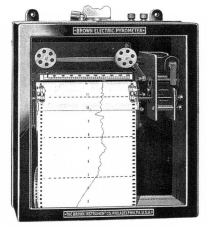

19

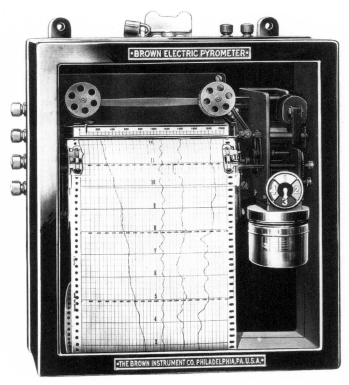

20

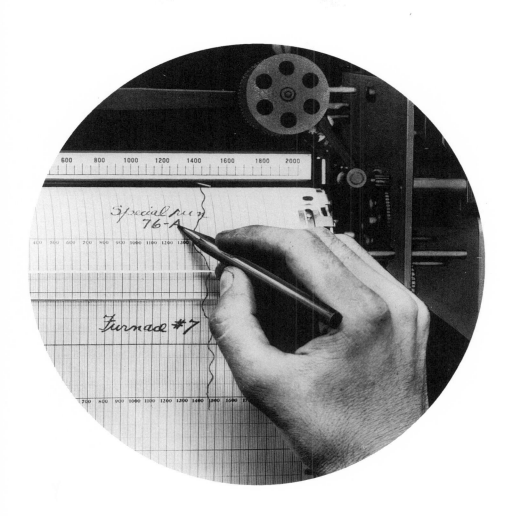

The student's dilemma is that of extent versus intensity. In 1907 I achieved the distinction of being the only student flunked in Josiah Penniman's course in the history of literary criticism. So far as I know I was the only student who was making any attempt to understand the subject of literary criticism and the only student with any interest in the subject save that of registering a certain number of credits toward an higher degree. So far as I know none of the other students have ever emerged from anonymity or appeared as literary critics in even the most humble degree.

I resigned from other literary courses because it seemed to me that the quantity of material one was expected or "told" to read was so infinitely in excess of the quantity, one could in the given time possibly read with any thought or real understanding.

Obviously one can not read everything. If one does not read enough, one's sense of general literary geography may suffer. It is better, however, to understand the one book in front of one than to have a superficial knowledge that it belongs in such and such a place. One might be fairly safe with a very few books if one kept oneself aware that they were not the whole of art and letters.

One's final judgment is "intuitive"? Or shall I say one's final judgment is made up of a certain number of formulatable reasons and a certain penumbra of imponderabilia.

Everything that I write on this subject must be taken with the context of Gourmont's *Physique de l'Amour* and of Fenollosa's essay on *The Chinese Written Character*. In Gourmont's exposition the instinct is not something opposed to intellect. Intellect is a sort of imperfect forerunner. After the intellect has worked on a thing long enough the knowledge becomes faculty. There is one immediate perception or capacity to act instead of a mass of ratiocination.

In art the *Kundiger*, the knower, is not the man who can analyze a work after it has been done; but the man who can go on from that work and do something different (different however slightly and with respect to whatsoever component he may happen to alter).

Dr. Réné Taupin in his book on French influences in contemporary American poetry has given the following exposition [. . .] I should suggest the following formulation as an improvement or if you like as a sign of where we have got to in our struggle against "abstraction," abstract terms, ideas that are merely "imperfect inductions from fact." A real thought (Leibnitzian monad of thought; ever active, incapable of being compressed out of existence, etc.) as distinct from a mere cliché or imperfect verbal manifestation consists of a pattern or group of related images; and this relation can be either in nature before the thought, or it can be the arbitrary relation thrust on the images by the man thinking.

As I now formulate this, A.D. 1930, I might simply be taking over a ready-made or half-made idea from the Gestaltists, though I am *not* even sure that they have suggested this group-image in relation to thought. As nearly as I can remember, "they" or some writer on Gestaltism has made the postulate in regard to biology or "something of that sort."

In one sense the division goes back as far as Abelard and the row between realists and nominalists. It is obviously related (faintly) to a remark of Aristotle's on the nature of metaphor.

Autobiographically, it derives from Fenollosa's essay on *The Chinese Written Character*, which profound and estimable essay I quite unwillingly had for my private and isolated instruction for several years, despite my best efforts to drill it into editorial heads, a series of editorial heads thicker than the walls of Sheol and filled with an undifferentiated cauliflower pulp or some similar substance.

It has now been in print for 12 years in the files of "The Little Review," and for 10 in my *Instigations*. For several years it has been out of print in both of these places and I am at loss to know whether I should give away the main point for three ha'pence or insist on the "public's" remaining in its natural state save when capable of hunting for the comparatively ungetatable founts. Or (in last ditch) howling for a reprint of the essay.

I have more recently pointed out that we are flooded with fake thought, not only in yellow journalism but in a new menace: scholastic journalism, i.e., works with scholastic titles and exterior which are made to meet the demands of a moribund system of scholarship and which commit the same peccadilloes as penny-a-liners. Of course the scholastics don't get a penny a line; they get, or hope for, a sort of scholastical as it were or ecclesiastical preferment. And with them is the phobosopher still bawling or squeaking abstractions (hammering his consumptive chest with a fist the size of a walnut).

And I have also pointed out that we are now quite well able to think things which do not fit the language as dolled up to meet the needs of monolinear logic.

Perhaps the overwhelming dullness of philosophy since Fr. Bacon is due to the fact that after Bacon's formulation (necessity for scientific research, etc.) there was really nothing more to be said, i.e., there was no need, or scarcely any need, for verbal manifestation *until* the intervening centuries of biological, chemical, physical experiments had been performed.

Descartes' verbal formulations are poor; his analytical geometry is magnificent.

And from the 16th Century onward philosophers have been valuable mainly in so far as they stuck to the sciences. When they are concerned with anything else, they still show the taint of Aristotle and Aquinas (the disease for our purposes is identical).

The biologist obviously knows a number of things for which he has no verbal manifestation and his knowledge is obviously untransmittable by verbal formulation. L. Berman goes so far as to deny that medical knowledge exists to men who have merely worked in laboratories and not actually practiced medicine.

However platitudinous my present formulation the thing I am driving at is not platitude. Properly understood it can be as important for the individual having patience enough to hunt for a meaning, as important for the actual thinking to come as was Bacon's formulation for the extension of scientific knowledge.

I have also offered the patient reader an acid which will free him from entanglements of a hundred and a thousand fake-thinkers. It is not merely in semi-serious criticism that these people abound. The whole of alleged philosophical and critical writing is riddled with malpractice. Every five years a new crop of people, some with scholastic labels and some without, strata selling the goods with a shifted trade mark, the same old shoddy.

The distinction is very simple; Fenollosa stated it very clearly, but either his essay was 32 pages long, or it didn't have a union label on it, or the title was "unfortunate" and Chinese writing an exotic. (Giambattista Vico's thought was not immediately perceived either, he came at things from his own angle.)

All of which paragraphs are merely oratorical device on my part. An attempt to isolate one paragraph of Fenollosa's, surround it with half-watt lights, underline it, etc. (failing which the printer may at his pleasure insert a little border of printer's bigs, roses and violets):

"Ask an occidental what red is and he will tell you that red is a colour; and ask him what colour is, and he will tell you colour is a refraction of light. Skip refraction and ask him what light is and he will tell you that it is a vibration of something or other, and ask him what vibration or other or electro-magnetism is and he will plunge still further into incognita. When, on the other hand, a Chinese man wishes to write down the ideograph for red he puts together the sign pictures for: cherry, rose, iron-rust and flamingo."

Fenollosa goes on to say that this latter is the method of science. He also draws several conclusions which are of infinite value when applied to "style," and he is thinking of poetic style in particular.

If the intelligent reader exists and if this falls under his eye he will stop for a few moments and think about it. And he will according to the vividness or coherence of his mind or according to his capacity for intellectual continuity draw, and at intervals thereafter continue to draw a number of inferences and if incapable of drawing them for himself, it would be futile for me to present him with a partial catalogue, which indeed he might "use" and with which he would make himself the same kind of damned nuisance that various persons have of themselves made and will make in times past, now and to come.

One can leave those bits of meteorite lying about in perfect safety, no one will steal them, the peaks of Parnassus will never be crowned.

Nineteen twenty-nine, ten years or so after I had forced Fenollosa's essay into print, I after a good deal of unpleasantness also forced an essay of my own into print. It contained a still stronger acid against the critical gonococcus. My serum was compounded of Fenollosa and of elements I had had in my tubes for still longer. The title of the essay was *How to Read*; it is about to undergo reprint. I wish by this present broadside to indicate the relation to Fenollosa's essay.

We are stifled with those pseudocritical essays in which one can insert a negative every ten lines without in any way indicating to any reader who doesn't know the subject beforehand whether the author is telling truth or falsehood.

A current method of writing allows an ignorant pretentious peda-
gogue to go on for forty pages without really displaying his imbecility,
whereas if one demanded his ideograph of let us say literary quality
at the start, one would know him at once for a mere bag of pom-
posity.

I have given the term "ideograph" a clearer and distinct definition
in *How to Read* and need not at this point repeat it.

The idea that the critic or philosopher should construct such an ideograph before demanding serious attention will not be popular with 80%
of the people now writing "critical articles," but it would or should be
extremely welcome to those who are interested in thought or in their
own particular subjects.

We can also with advantage distinguish between the selective or critical faculty and the capacity for, or habit of, producing "finished critical articles." The faculty and the capacity are not mutually exclusive,
neither are they invariably found together.

The danger of starting merely a new academicism either from such a
table of prohibitions or cautions, or from a table of authors and works
recommended, or from both can only be avoided by balancing them
against a sense of possibility and of defect.

In this year 1930 we are or should be faced with the perception that
means of literary expression have fallen behind science.

I mean that the scientist, say the biologist, knows a great many things
for which there is no proper and ready verbal manifestation. He falls
back on photos and coloured slides. His need of accurate "description"
is greater than extant language can satisfy.

And this crisis should carry us "either as readers or writers," though
perhaps chiefly and certainly firstly as writers, such of us as are readers
and certainly such of us as are writers to a closer consideration of the
nature of language.

That is to say L. Bruhl, the savage with his wood and river; where the
biologist is in New York in 1930 with his cells (is at first sight) in relation to language. Or in relation to cells re[garding] in re[ference] to
language. Generalization next phase.

The concrete knowledge precedes the generalization; and the generalization; and the generalization only absorbs a very small part of the real knowledge, one thread out of the tangle.

Hence the capacity for extremely ignorant people knowing a great deal and remaining quite stupid. All the difference between knowing that Charleston is the capital of South Carolina and having lived in the place 20 years.

It must be clear to anybody that will think about the matter for 15 minutes that reading a good author in a foreign tongue will joggle one out of the cliches of ones own and will as it were scratch up the surface of one's vocabulary. I take today's example. "Man lives . . . in engster *Verkampfung* mit der ihn umgeberden Natur."

I have said in a dozen places that two races do not think out the same set of things. The sets ever cross; they are handed down from mutual ancestors etc. . . . The two races do not think the same things in the same way. The Jap who appears to us vague in certain ideas is "vague" merely because his categories cut in a different way. An individual with clear form categories may be vague in colour. As an eastern rug maker will have colour categories finer than that of a "great" European painter or "colourist."

All this goes down into language. The most immediately handy may be the one nearest our own. It may be French that has common ancestry and from which we have borrowed directly.

The language is the thesaurus, but the heritage is not of one commodity only. There is the vocabulary, there is the idiom, and there is the technique and the art of writing.

English has a richer vocabulary, for example, than French. That is not to say that there has been *no* development in German language or technique or that a German would not notice very marked differences between the verse of Stefan Georg and Rilke, but these differences are by no means so fundamental or general as those in French. They do not give anything like the same stimulus to the foreigner. There are thirty unknown poets in France who have innovated probably as greatly as Rilke without attracting notice. This is not to say that they are great poets or will go down to posterity. Merely in the general speed their pace is not remarkable; whereas in the German pace Rilke's speed attracts notice.

As comment the reader can compare the fine verse in Burckhardt's translation of the *Vita Nuova* with his original verse. Where he has a mediaeval Mediterranean Latin content before him the Teuton speech adds and alters something and the result is admirable. It appears to me that these processes parallel those that produced Minnesang in Vogelweide, etc. Dates of German mediaeval poets are very early and will jolt anyone who thinks that they were copying known Provençal poets.

Monos convenience in some lines of thought.

Effect on people rotten; ought not to be accepted *unless* so.

Certain and obvious disadvantage. All the vileness of our time Calvin; to age of Coleridge; Volsted; Byron etc. bare thought; fanaticism.

Interference of the vacuous with others traceable to this root.

If it were a scientific or revealed truth, one thing; but as it is merely an hypothesis, no.

Formula of humanism long since "given": *mens sana in corpore sano.* There is resaying this in ten volumes or blah.

The *corpore sano* implies sensibility, balance etc. also an awareness of the present. The *mens* implies also Gestalt, or the extension of Gestalt formula to time.

The higher the physical development, the more complicated the Gestalt (space); the higher the *mens*, the longer the durée.

Shaving down of durée to infinitesimals or mere sequence flow (Bertie) etc. not an advance.

The relativity in highest—*mens*—

is that Bach might be conceived as conceiving a whole fugue in an instant; probably no composer ever did; but these foreshortenings or instantaneous conceptions and knowings of Gestalt that in expression needs extension in time are the indicated highest *mens*. Not chipchopping into uniformity.

The demon of our age is uniformity, mediaeval theological dissociation of ideas better than in post-Baconian soup.

A Protestant nun from India and a returned Chinese missionary, that is to say two people who have transported a set of ready made ideas eastward, and who have been as we would say monkeying with the orient, rummaging or stirring about in the wreckage and rubbish of the oriental past, ask me abruptly what I mean by civilization.

After hemming and hawing, I am able 24 hours later to decide that civilization is a social order in which the more active, constructive, and finely perceptive intelligences are permitted to act with reasonable freedom, free from inane impediments, and in which they do actually cooperate or at least mutually irritate and stimulate each other.

This might of course occur even in what could be called a social disorder. But the disorder would have to be to some extent moderated.

These general definitions are too indefinite. One can not think without the concrete instance.

Civilization does in some way persist through the net of degrading idiocy and fanaticisms which seems to be preferred at all times by the more loathsome and disgusting part (often the majority) of mankind or of a particular nation.

Gongorism and the new Gongorism merely belong to that general category in which the brilliancy or salience of particular details obscures the main theme or motivation.

Decadent art, I think all decadent art without exception is art in which the detail receives or demands too much attention against the main subject.

I don't know whether the main subject can get too much attention. If it does, the art is primitive or great or possibly crude, but in the latter case it probably hasn't even any intention of being art at all, etc.

But there is nothing in English properly comparable to the experimentation in French poetry of the last seventy years, etc.

When we break out of European languages and the Renaissance tradition, we get still stronger alternatives. Notably the ideograph and in a less significant way the languages studied by Lévy-Bruhl.

But even in German we get this jolt of the man buttoned into surrounding nature, and this in sober prose that is not trying to cummings. (I use cummings here as a verb.)

Every language has absorbed into itself and made common metaphors that were at their origin probably just as startling and fancy as the wildest tropes of our contemporary eccentrics.

The good writer takes them when they are "right," when they are hard enough for his purpose, and tough so that they will not crumble.

The great style is without preoccupations and bothers concerning detail. Its unity is in the thought underlying and in the modality of that thought prepared by the thinker's past life. "C'est l'homme," etc. Recognition of this dates back to at least Confucius.

It can only be faked for Chitaqua and for the ladies club audience or an "electorate."

Addenda (c. 1928–1936)

I.

I wish once more to assert that Ernest Fenollosa's essay on *The Chinese Written Character* is a very valuable piece of writing, especially for anyone interested in the foregoing treatise. Due to the idiocy and blockheadness of a number of editors and publishers I have enjoyed the privilege of knowing the Fenollosa essay for some years before it was available to others. (In which connection let me again state for the general scandal that I would cheerfully raise from the dead a certain P. Carus if I might thereby have the pleasure of kicking him [in] the stomach. For stupidity in not understanding Fenollosa and for incivility in holding up the mss. for a year or so he may be taken as typical of a certain contemptible type of editor who deserves some sort of permanent pillory. We are too patient with such and more of them should be held up to infamy.)

II.

The next "movement" in literature, or shall we say the problem upon which the best writers are already engaged is that of carrying into literature the advantages of science. By which I do not mean using literature to argue about scientific discovery.

In the middle ages abstract terminology achieved a great virtuosity; today on the contrary the biologist can think many things, can know many things which he finds it quite impossible to convey by language. He formulates laws etc. etc., but a knowledge of his terminology is not a knowledge of biology. The syllogism is of next to no value.

He recognizes a dozen different tissues and states of tissue by a complex of perceptions for which language gives him no expression or at least no synthetic expression. Familiarity with the perceived complex of visual or sensuous data by the scientist must inevitably beget something more apt for its conveyance than is the simple monolinear sentence.

The first efforts will be largely mess. And the imitation of the serious experimentor's results by faddists and impressionable people who have not the *slightest* idea of what the investigator is up to, will doubtless provide a marvellous pullulation of (with apologies for the metaphor) hog-wash.

I don't mean that language will be a substitute for the photographed micro-slide or the coloured reproduction in biological study; but that the *kind* of knowledge current in science must beget a demand for similarly accurate thought both in material science and in regard to the general consciousness, with analogous complexity and synthesis in expression. The simple formula "man sees horse" can not serve indefinitely for all purposes. Nor, I think, can even the H. Jamesian sentence.

We are also due for a mass of silly criticism from those who fail to discriminate between incomparably valuable experiment and the achieved and ultimate masterwork.

I can perhaps emphasize my meaning best by saying that if a 15 year old boy told me he wanted to write and asked the best form of training I should tell him to proceed gradually along the lines of my outline; so far as mere reading of literary works is concerned, but to spend [the] major part of his time . . . to study medicine or biology; zoology; and to read the books in my list in his spare time.

"To understand things in their natural colours and relations"

infinitely more use to a writer than any prolonged immersion in other men's work.

Stupid not to know Homer, and to have some standard of criticism of verbal manifest[ation]; but a technique is not of expression, comes with use.

Some one had to make the general survey that I have made and recorded. But had someone else done it first, I hope I would have had sense enough to study some science; not an "abstract one" for the writer's job but some science of living organism.

Better subjugate poetry to an aspiring than an expiring political party or doctrine *i.e.* to say bolshevism or fascio than to one merely advocating existing swindles, oppressions etc. But the idea of subjugating it, or the arts to any blooming or fading doctrine, is bunk. Or rather a limitation.

Art dealing, as science does, with things which subsist, which outlast any party or creed, which are here under capita, and will be here or would be here, under communism, fascio, or anything else.

Neither Lenin or anyone else having power to change one's endocrine composition.

If you like, art is a part of biology. Not a minion of social conventions or human arrangements.

Art for art's sake, no, art for propaganda, no, art is part of biology.

As to the spreading, publishing of it, of good literature the party that publishes the best, is in the long run the triumphant party. The enlightened, the unopposable party.

Language is here to serve thought.

It is not something to be preserved in a museum. The Italian language is in need of sand paper.

There are two exotics, such as the American school of Montparnasse, that is, those who want to be exotic; and those who import useful and necessary things.

Language must serve thought: where there is no thought; where there is no strong thought, there is no need of novelty or expression. Fake thought thus betrays itself.

The American or English or Christian morality is dastardly because it is a lie; it is false.

Greek mythology and science alike show us not a strife between a good and a bad but a conflict of forces and inertias, a conflict of different necessities and modalities; each good or in certain degree.

The moral problem is not so simple; it is not merely bilateral.

Il y a plusieurs plans.
   Relation biological, not syllogistic;
there is a great deal of relation, correlation.
Syllogistic relation does not exist between natural phenomena. Any-

how, poor sort of rapport, never more than one dimension to it, or
hardly ever.

1932

FOR THE BENEFIT of these people who keep asking for a "meaning"
when what they want is an impoverishment of the meaning.

I am NOT offering them a few miserable obiter dicta about the cosmos. (Which is what they call "a philosophy.")

I am not offering a "system of thought" if that means a few *idées fixes*
arranged in a pattern on a shelf.

I offer a system of thinking.

Any biologist will understand you if you say mankind is my bug.

General protest against the widely prevalent, but never openly acknowl-
edged attitude of the scholastics, that works written in exuberance
should be approached in a spirit of sobriety or even of gloom.

The object or at least one object of reading is to prevent oneself from
being bamboozled, by cranks, by fixed and petrified ideas and modes of
thought, by the naiveté of rationalization, especially by the trick of the
syllogism and by the unexpected occurrence.

It might seem unnecessary to reprint some of these early notes but, if
the thought in these papers has any value, it has been largely as a con-
secutive process and not merely picking daisies at random. The method
was already there in 1908. It culminates in the discrimination of "ideogrammic method" after Fenollosa's essay, but that essay is not here
without reason. Mrs. Fenollosa did not hand over her husband's papers
to the first academic idiot with a knowledge of pidgin. She had kept
them for several years (1908 to 1913) until I met her at Sarojini Naidu's
and had considered them if not as a sacred trust at any rate as a very
serious trust, and gave them to me because she had found in my writing
qualities which led her to believe that I would edit and present them as
Ernest Fenollosa had wished.

All of which will not surprise people holding certain beliefs. At any
rate I am contending that a method exists and that the method can cure
certain forms of critical grossness, particularly that of letting in every
grubby-handed professor to muddle art with pseudo-philosophy. The

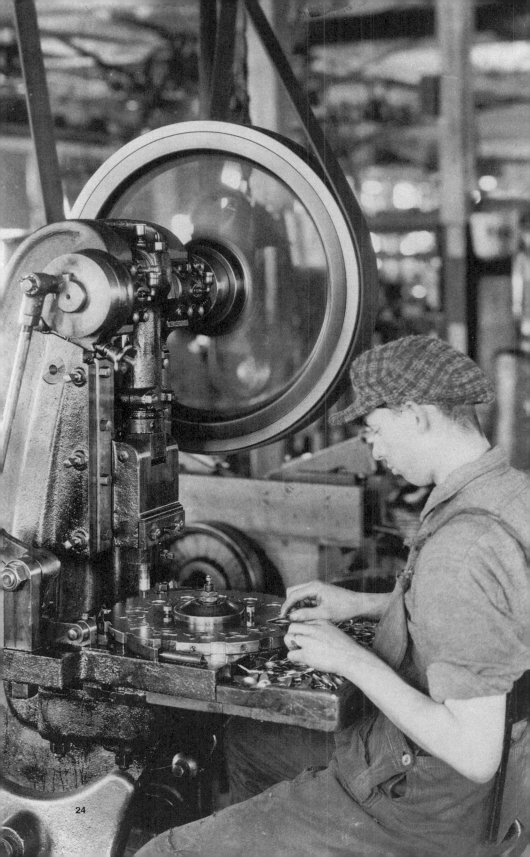

24

25

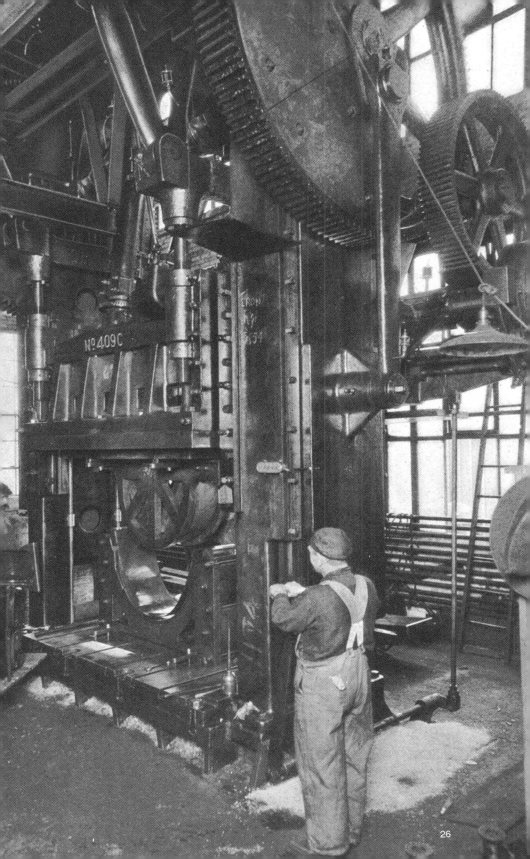

grossness of the *vulgus* is in never being able to isolate any subject of discussion. Incapable of treating philosophy as philosophy or art as art, incapable of defining an idea as such, ignorant of philosophy as they are, ignorant of art, they write smearing now of one now of the other, usually camouflaging their own addled apperception by trying to foist it onto some author whom they have misunderstood or not troubled to apprehend. Ignorant of language and of music, they drag in metaphysics, though they would not and possibly could not discuss metaphysics or physics with anyone trained in philosophical dialectic or exact science of observation.

The patient reader can, I think, find the root of the ideogrammic method in the notes first published in the *Egoist* under the title *The Serious Artist* (1913).

The actual employment of it has already begun in the *I Gather the Limbs of Osiris* (1911–1912).

Them 'Eavy Thinkers

"Opponents of Darwin, such as Edmund Gosse's father, urged a very similar argument against evolution. The world, they said, was created in 4004 B.C. complete with fossils, which were inserted to try our faith. There is no logical impossibility about this view."

Thus Mr. B. Russell, giving us a very just measure of what "logic" or what is so called among present professors of philosophy means or implies. Observe that dear Bertrand has not arrived at page six of his "Outline" without previously committing terminological inexactitude (on p. 5) that would have scandalized a freshman of A.D. 1250, but still thank him for his apparatus.

The scientist and the better of the literati have long since chucked belief in the syllogistic mechanism. The professed philosopher, so long as he is occupied merely in bickering over the verbal formulae to be used for definition of certain perfectly familiar states of ignorance, may cling to his superstitions. It is time "logic" will have to pull up its socks, chucking the old classroom hocus-pocus need not mean definite retirement of "logic" from the field of existence.

Of course we all know what Mr. Russell means by "no logical impossibility," but he should learn to express his meaning before producing any more books, or burdening us with further expression.

The fault of Russell and his contemporary colleagues is, generally, gross verbal inexactitude, as the fault of Aquinas (and his crew) is in the multitude [of] utterly unwarranted assumptions. From which two causes it happens that neither gang has been of any great use, and that their modes of manifestation have not contributed to the advancement of science or been of any appreciable benefit to humanity.

In deciding what man has caused the greatest waste of human time, Aristotle must be considered among the more prominent candidates.

What Mr. Pound believes a response to Mr. Eliot's questions

Profound? go down down down till you jump thru your owne anus and when you come out the other side and onto IT; *it is alive.*

That is the splendour of the cosmos.

That is probably what Mr. Leibnitz swatted at with his "monad."

Since Leibnitz there has been no theology, and no philosophy. That is to say, there have been essays on philosophic subjects, but the *thought* has been a mere weak derivative from scientific discovery.

IT IS ALIVE. It says nothing about not fishing on Sunday or about having only one woman or about fealty to the constitution.

Whenever a scientist has come into contact with the practice of hired economists he has been both amazed and disgusted. A "science" which excluded facts from its field of investigation and demonstration is not rated very high among physicists, biologists, chemists.

"Orthodox" economy, is in fact not a science, it is scholasticism. The phenomena are the world war, and poverty. These things do not enter the "orthodox" calculations.

A science? that excludes phenomena from its own domain.

That excludes so much real knowledge from its domain, that enquires into nothing inconvenient, and treats its own conventions as if they were phenomena of nature, or even laws of the cosmos.

Philosophy from time of Leibnitz has been a series of undigested almost uncorrelated reflexions from the discoveries in material science.

Not attracted the best brains, or been most alert or been very alert even in taking hold of the thought and formulations of other sciences and particular fields, fields of research.

Antisocial communists, communists with no sense of the commune. Men too lazy to learn the system under which they live. Economic studies.

Agin neo-religiousism. There is the consciousness which is a mystery, vegetables, animal life, mysteries. All modern man has to say regarding one religious problem vs other is that he approves its attitude towards some given reality.

April 1936
Religion to be religion at all must claim a higher place than philosophy. Philosophy to be philosophy must concern itself with universal principles. Philosophy since the time of Leibniz has been the poor weak trailer after material science.

But a religion or a philosophy whose principles can only apply to a fraction of human relationships is a contradiction in terms. In other words only nit-wits can be deceived into taking such camouflage for solid.

In a country where rank intellectual cowardice is so nearly universal that any sign of intellectual courage or honesty passes for eccentricity, it maybe seems unlikely that either religion or philosophy would get very far.

Nature of mind to move, of matter to stop; of mind to be incapable of conceiving a limit whereat stop is possible, tho' wisdom to circumscribe action or consideration of action, the practicability of a "field"; but in consideration of matter the moment mind gets "into it," i.e., into the consideration begins to discover potentials and dynamisms, as p.e. in atom.

Any man in state of dense ignorance can write reams of such general reflections, mere prelude of thinking.

Honesty of the Word Does Not Permit Dishonesty of the Matter

If in my early criticism I showed just contempt for the falsity of writer who would not face technical problems that cannot pass, for much longer, as indifference to *ethos* or to values of any kind. An artist's technique is a test of his personal validity. Honesty of the word is the writer's first aim, for without it he can communicate nothing efficiently, but velleities may be of no more avail than that of blue blurred men howling for peace, while abetting the murderers and mass starvers.

Orthology is a discipline both of morale and of morals.

Value of Style

Without *le mot juste*, without exact expression, the fitting of right word to the thing, no truth can exist, a man can neither communicate with another, nor can he present the truth to himself, or get his ideas into any sort of sound order.

The D.M. almost unmitigated evil, a medium in which no truth can exist. Even if writer wishes to make true statement the statement he does make is applicable to so much else.

In good writing the words arise from the thing; in bad they are canalization, the phrase arises from the accustomed phrase, the easy worn groove of speech.

Without just style, expression, no clear idea, no law, no society having a decent order, no amenity, no clean relations with things, ideas, or people.

Respect for honest writers, and contempt for the defilers.

A Problem of (Specifically)
Style (1934)

Even the death of the last survivors of the clogging and war-causing generation that preceded us, will not bring a new and illumined era unless at least the élite of ours or (that being unlikely) the next, make some effort to understand the function of language, and to understand why a tolerance for slipshod expression in whatever department of writing gradually leads to chaos, munitions-profiteers, the maintenance of wholly unnecessary misery, omnipresent obfuscation of mind, and a progressive rottenness of spirit.

Mr. Eliot in advocating a species of Christianity has, so far as I am aware, neglected to define religion. His readers are befogged as to whether he wants a return to the Christian Church (as it was in the year Sixteen Hundred, in Chiswick) or whether he wants us to turn religious, or in what order.

There *is* a distinct difference in Anschauung between men who believe that the world needs religion and those who believe it needs some particular brand or flavour of religion.

Among professionals, that is, men who get their board and keep by religion, it is to-day almost impossible to find any really professional competence in theology. I have yet to find a professor or religious writer who has bothered to formulate a definition of "religion" before touting his own particular brand. George Washington, refusing to be cornered and driven into profession of belief in an undefined something or other, commended the "beneficent influence of the Christian Religion."

Given an effect, even the most agnostic and merely logical mind will admit a cause.

Given the necessity of volition, the freest thinker might admit the necessity or advisability of a direction of that volition.

Given an increasing awareness that there exists circumvolving us a vast criminal class that never infringes any "law" on the statute book or breaks an enforceable police regulation, the more perceptive tend in some cases to believe in the usefulness of a "general disposition," you might even say they incline toward a belief in the need of a general disposition, toward the Whole, the cosmos, and even toward the consciousness inherent in that cosmos.

No man is aware of that consciousness save via his own, but believing in a great telephone central or not or in minor centrals or not, no scientist can deny at least fragmentary portions of consciousness which have a sum, a totality, whether or not they have coherent inter-organisation.

The minute a man takes into consideration the totality of this universe, or the sum of this consciousness, he has, whether he wants it or not, a religion. And some phase of that consciousness is his theos: whether coherent or non-coherent, labile, intermittent or whatever.

And into his thought and action there enters a component influence affecting, in all degrees from the infinitesimal up to 100%, his volition, and his specific acts or the general tone of his action.

Religion in humanist terms would be valuable in the degree in which it directed a man toward the welfare of humanity (judged not necessarily in mere terms of eating, but also in terms of mental condition, peace of mind, mental vitality).

Granting that mankind may need a religion; that, in concrete instances, many men will—so long as they lack one—do nothing that seems to me to be of the faintest use or of the faintest possible interest, I should have to have some evidence that the given professional had reason for touting his own particular brand in preference to any three dozen others; and such evidence would have to come to me, either from a greater efficiency in good action or greater mental clarity and honesty as displayed in his manifest thought. Thought to be manifest would have to be so, either by verbal expression or by demonstration in some other sensible medium.

A manifest funking of straight thought or honest action in any specific field falling under one's examination, would obviously throw out the fakers, i.e., it would obviously bring any brand of religion into disrepute with thoughtful observers, whether this applied to an individual exponent or to an "organisation."

The Medieval Church in its wisdom placed excessive sloth among sins. In no field has the sloth of our time been more foul and oppressive than in the search for clear terminology. In no field has England been more damned than in failing to dissociate ideas.

In all fields this muddiness is so great that any field serves as repulsive example; and among all morasses the economic morass is the dankest.

Experts representing their nations in international congresses are no better than timorous instructors holding their jobs on sufferance and fearing for the food of their offspring.

Lacking a religion or a decent ethical base, there is no reason why Bug'ush and Co. shouldn't be content in creating confusion. Lacking an ethical base there is no argument against the perpetual (as I see it) infamy of dragging discussion continually onto the unessential, and continually away from the search after truth and knowledge.

If scientists are not always free from a personal vanity, we have at least proof that in the laboratories a great number of men do search after biological and chemical knowledge without being continually led off into personal bickerings, petty struggles for precedence. Medical science does and a number of medical scientists do set an example, however many fools may have on dramatic occasions tried to obstruct a medical hero.

In no science can truth go forward when men are more anxious to show up another man's minor error, or to prove his failure of fool-proof formulation, than to use his perception of truth (however fragmentary) for a greater perception and for the formulation of valid equations.

We were, manifestly, drug up analphabetic in economics. We are manifestly surrounded by an ignorance of economic history which sheds infamy on every college and university and shows up the whole congeries of economic professors as apes with the rarest possible exception.

We lack any organisation for the publication and correlation of economic studies. Jeffry Mark's last book, "The Modern Idolatry," is invaluable, however fragmentary, and if we need a dozen more, of similar sort, at least this can be set up as an ad interim scaffolding.

Or on the other hand a member of Bug'ush and Co. has recently tried to obscure Douglas's very profound observation that you need not issue all credit as debt. He has found a very clever sophistry; that all debt is somebody's credit. The vital question would seem to be, Whose?

I take it young Juggins would admit a difference between a debt he owed a man who did not want usury, and a note on which he was paying interest?

I take it also that at whichever end you look at it, a debt or credit is frozen when the debtor is unable to pay?

I take it that the Social Credit formulators (and I myself for that matter) might have prevented young Juggins's quibble had we asked: Why issue all new credit as debt with interest?

But that would not have enlightened young Juggins as to the fountain of value, or opened his mind to the fact that a state *has credit.*

Does Juggins, when *he* has credit, write it down as debt? Does he at once start paying interest on it to Messrs. X, Q, and N?

I take it he does not, but I would like him to answer the question: Does the "increment of association" mean anything in their philosophy? Have they a philosophy?

Does the "heritage" figure in their computation?

Does the increment of associated machinery carry a meaning into their consciousness?

Do they still sup with Brother Barr and dream of hoisting up water-buckets by hand, or of "devising employment" for millions of unemployable people who would like to eat better and whose food would cost us so much less than their employment?

Ogden and Debabelization (1935)

If mere extensions of vocabulary, or use of foreign words is a sin, I surely am chief among all sinners living. Yet, to the best of my knowledge, I have never used a Greek word or a Latin one where English would have served. I mean that I have never intentionally used, or wittingly left unexpurgated, any classic or foreign form save where I asserted: this concept, this rhythm is so solid, so embedded in the consciousness of humanity, so durable in its justness that it has lasted 2,000 years, or nearly three thousand. When it has been an Italian or French word, it has asserted or I have meant it to assert some meaning not current in English, some shade or gradation.

Jefferson, who spent a half century in public life, and who began with a fine sense of legal precision; has left us the clearest measure for the use of neologism, and one that casts out diddlers and twiddlers. The new word or unsanctified term was justified when it conveyed something that could not be in other wise conveyed.

None of my own readers, and I think none of the most postulant of my opponents, will suspect me of prejudice in favour of a restricted vocabulary. If I am Ogden's ally I am probably the last one he looked for.

My recent condensed recommendation for Social Credit Policy was as follows:

1. Simplification of Terminology.

2. Articulation of terminology ("distinguish the root from the branch").

3. AS MUCH PROPAGANDA AS POSSIBLE SHOULD BE WRITTEN IN BASIC ENGLISH.

4. Less intolerance toward converging movements.

5. Hammer on root ideas.

6. Speakers and writers should bear in mind the black ignorance of the public and tell each separate audience that:

(1) Money is not a commodity.

(2) Work is not a commodity.

(3) The State *has* credit.

(4) The increment of association exists (explain what it is).

(5) Cultural Heritage: increment of association with all past inventiveness, the FOUNT from which State dividends are payable.

I am very much in earnest about the third specification. I don't in the least imagine any of us will be able to compose straight off in basic. I do not suggest that any man should hamper himself in the immensely difficult job of exact expression, or in the still more highly technical activity of clause 2, by worrying about any linguistic limitations whatsoever.

For three decades I have believed, taught and practised that translation is the absolute best among all forms of writer's training. When the translation is made into a castigated and tried segment of the mother tongue itself, that training is, or can be, intensified.

The fall of mediaeval culture took thought out of the grip of writers and speakers. From the death of Leibniz till today, no philosophic thought came into being save as trailer after material science. Social Credit itself has been delayed because Douglas had a more thorough training in engineering than in language.

The "Betrayal of the Clerks" is real as it is flagrant. For the tenth time of repeating it: when thought tackled matter, when it, thank heaven, spread from the control of the verbalists, into the domain of chemical experimentation, optics as proved in practice, etc., the new precision, which lay in direct observation, which was not and could not be transmitted by phrases, left language to sunbake and decompose. Before the stink of capital and the beastly practices of the publishing trade had got into language further to putrify and corrupt it, a deterioration had already set in.

Mediaeval logic did at least discipline the contemplative in the uses and modes of language. Parts of speech were not interchanged. A verb took things out of eternity, and located them somewhere in time (*quod significat tempus*). The appalling bog of words in Wells, Chesterton, to take the mighty, and in the whole welter and foetor slobbering down through the American professors and magazine mugs, down to absolute bottom in Middleton Murry, is a nauseous spectacle, whence rises a piercing cry for cloacae.

Ogden, and his once partner Richards, have offered us at any rate a few sturdy duck-boards, a dry footing, wherefrom to conduct our operations.

I see three uses of BASIC.

I. As training and exercise, especially for excitable yeasty youngsters who want so eagerly to mean something that they can't take out time to think: What?

II. As sieve. As a magnificent system for measuring extant works. As a jolly old means of weeding out bluffs, for weeding out fancy trimmings, and leaving Kipling and Hardy possibly somewhat improved. If a novelist can survive translation into basic, there is something solid under his language.

There is nothing Philistine in this suggestion. The inferiority of the Basic rendering of "Mistress Mine where are you roving" to the original, will pluck no feather from Avon's swan. But the wreckage of the Amy Lowell, the outsluicing of Georgian hogwash will be a sight passing tatto'd ladies.

III. This is our specific opportunity: the advantages of BASIC vocabularly limited to 850 words and their variants, plus the specific technical vocabulary for individual sciences, for the diffusion of ideas is, or should be, obvious to any man of intelligence.

BASIC is offered as a second and supplementary language. Its immeasurable superiority to all languages invented ab initio is that it already has a full racy idiom, comprehensible to hundreds of millions of people. As means of transmission it is, obviously, superior to the "Times" fog or the "Manchester Guardian" twitter.

And in postscript. No science has such need of a rigorous discipline as has economics in the year 1935.

If Mr. Ogden thinks I have omitted anything, I trust he will augment this statement. I trust, in any event, he will take the opportunity to state his own case, and at length, in these pages.

European Paideuma

European Paideuma (1940)

To hell with Spengler! In Europe lie the sources of the valid elements of our cultural inheritance. What we believe is European — and by no means in a state of Untergang! In this essay I distinguish between intellect and intelligence. "Intellect" is the mental scaffolding which men erect to deal with what they do not understand. "Intelligence" is seeing, noting and accepting. Belief is from intelligence.

From the Baltic to the Mediterranean certain things are believed. Books serve only to obscure them. Our knowledge of these things should be implicit in our way of living. Unfortunately it is limited largely to such of them as have caught the eye of the more popular sort of folklorist. The Lithuanian shout of "Ligo" to a sun freed of its winter imprisonment, the maze-dances performed at Easter near Mycenae express an observance of, and belief in natural forces on which, ultimately, our whole existence depends. The changing seasons with all that they imply for us are the subject on the one hand of statistics, corners in wheat, planning commissions for the restriction of crops and Federal Relief (U.S.A.), on the other of observance, thankfulness, fear and a belief in the commonplace and ever-recurring miracle of growth.

The people of Rapallo rushing down into the sea on Easter morning or bringing their gardens of Adonis to church on the Thursday before have not learned these things in school.[1] Nor did they have them originally from Christian priests. The same thing is true of the silk cocoons

1. Shoots prematurely forced. The seeds are put on wet flannel, sprout early and are a part of the Easter decoration in the Rapallo churches.

27

which, during Easter Week, the peasant women bring to church care-fully concealed under their aprons.[2]

The whole of romance, the amour courtois of Provence, the Minne-sänger, mediaeval legend, the Venusberg and Tristan are ineradicable of belief. As are feasts of planting and harvest and feasts for the turn of the sun. Aphrodite, Adonis, Helios. Belief is in the writings of the Ghibelline poets. These same students, as the late L. Valli for example (*Linguaggio Segreto di Dante*) have intellectualized too far and have seen in what they thought were secret intentions things to which they did not have and could not have the key.

The for the present extremely unfashionable Swinburne had, I think, at one time, belief. ("Ballad of Life" and "Julian Apostate.") He also knew more Greek than any Englishman after the happy days of Porson and W. Savage Landor.

The Christian Church was of very mixed elements of which the valid were European. It was not long, however, before the (for us) invalid ele-ments (from the Near East) gained the upper hand. Implanted in its ter-

2. This custom is not a matter of common knowledge even in Rapallo.

minology, they overflowed Roman order and Roman concept, Roman graduation and Roman hierarchy—leaving a verbal mass so septic that the intelligent were poisoned.

There is no need here to go into details. It suffices to repeat here that fans used in high ceremonies are of Egyptian origin, that donning and doffing of mitres is phallic symbolism in Oriental clothing. The religious element is admittedly pagan, but mere paganism is not enough. The intellectual elements are Plato and Aristotle, the latter largely destructive of faith and belief—in the sense in which I have defined the word (intellect) in my first paragraph.

On the other hand the sea-board shrines to the Madonna delle Grazie[3] are not Oriental. These have most emphatically *not* come from Palestine. The Madonna of the Italian peasant is an *örtliche raumgebundene Gottheit*, a purely local divinity. She is THEIR Madonna, present in a given ambience. Moreover, the really vigorous feasts of the Church[4] are the European ones, those which existed before the Church and which will remain when the Church is forgotten: the feasts of the sun, of the harvest and of Aphrodite.

It is some four hundred years since the Church started on its path of moral and spiritual bankruptcy. For this usury and the revival of ancient Jewish texts (Old Testament) may, in part, have been responsible. Its decline began with a flight from reality. For it must have been fear that prompted it, in 1208, a century or so after the man's death, to exhume the bones of Scotus Erigena and to damn him as unbeliever. Scotus' crime had been his intelligence. For he had said "authority comes from right reason" and he had defined sin as "a lapse from reality." It may be said here that the followers of Confucius and of Mencius were horrified at the immoral and anti-social nature of Christianity and for a long time kept it out of China on those grounds. One may wish, and many good men have wished, to do honour to the intellectual structure built up by Rome from the time of St. Ambrose down to the Renaissance. Let us affirm again that the valid parts of this thought—such sanities and pro-

3. Sailor shrines at points commanding a view of the sea, for instance, that on Monte Allegro on the limestone heights above Rapallo. The shrines are filled with votive offerings of ship models and pictures of shipwrecks from which the votators have been saved. "Hang me bells in Venus' shrine."

4. Mr. Pound has suggested that more attention be paid to Ovid, a very serious compiler of known festivals.

portions as may be found in it—are Roman, the questionable intellectual framework is Athenian. Personally, I say: Up Greece! Damn Athens!

Because there are people who acknowledge that the Church is bankrupt it is ridiculous to assume that Europe is naturally without religion. That statement has been used by pacifiers and by impoverishers, by schizophrenics and by those who from questionable motives have wished to weaken Europe. It is a pity for the sake of our mental grasp that the delvers into religion have so often been led off into Buddhism, into Malthusianism or have flopped into Theosophy instead of sticking to a search for belief.

In the teeth of current snobisms I have pointed out that the German pavilion at last year's Venetian Biennial Exposition was the best pavilion there. Any visitor with an unperverted sense of form should have seen this. Failure to understand the new turn in the arts is due partly to dullness but even more to stultification through dealer-propaganda, something which has gone on with steady infection for at least fifty years.

Greek sculptors made gods; Romans, emperors; Italians of the Quattrocento, individuals. But all in a proper direction. Leonardo wanted to know true proportions—and so did Petrus de Burgo before him ("Prospectiva Pingendi," reprinted in Strasbourg in 1899). The Quattrocento is the most European century on record and even Botticelli is indisputably (100%) European. [. . .]

For our own information we must reinspect Leo Frobenius's graphs. It would be useful if the *Forschungsinstitut für Kulturmorphologie* gathered into one volume a brief list of the distinctly European beliefs encountered in the total mass of Frobenius' writings. Another useful contribution from the same source would be an analysis for the falsification and distortion of European belief. Vulcan into Thor, or vice-versa? Vulcan provided with a tail and made a part of Semitic mythology? With that and with a wholly new and vigorous examination of the Dionysus cult and of the Bacchic invasion we might be getting somewhere. [. . .]

Along with Frobenius' studies I offer my own notes on "Medievalism" in CAVALCANTI and my "Ethics of Mencius" (Criterion, July 1938). I should like to see my "Guide to Kulchur" (New York and London, 1939) in a German translation, no matter how chopped, allusive and unsatisfactory it may seem to systematic minds.

Convenit esse Deos (c. 1940–1942)

My emphasis is on the plural. Mr. Eliot in a recent number of one of our popular magazines, responding to or entering into argument with a name so freighted with dullness that I will not here burden the reader with repetition, advocates (mildly) a return to religion. So far as I can make out from his somewhat general terminology, religion means for him that pest of the Occident: monotheism, in some sort of mildly dry form. Perhaps I wrong him in this. Perhaps he does not suffer from the century long blight of the Occident.

A god in the singular is always lacking in temperance, in amenity, a god in the singular is on the whole a peril, an imminent nuisance. There is nothing in nature or in science to force one to assuming god in the singular. A god in the singular is a mental convenience for a certain type, not the best type, of hag-ridden mind. The chief hag being a sort of logical pinwheel, if this gongoristic metaphor is permitted me.

For the lack of gods (plural) man suffers, or let us say he very gradually impoverishes his mind by the elimination of irreplaceable concepts.

Semito-phobia is better explainable as semi-conscious revenge on the race that has brought monotheism into general European circulation than by any other single or complex set of reasons offered or yet offered.

A tendency which ends by offering the Salem ducking-stool for the myth of Daphne and Apollo is not a tendency friendly to the race, nor are the types (endocrine compounds) that cherish or propagate this tendency the best types for the racial welfare.

The sentence against Socrates was probably just; or rather in the long run it turns out to be in the process of justifying its original appearance of harshness. Not that the Socrates of Plato works his syllogism to

28

death. In fact the few bursts of intelligence in Plato's illogical, and re-
plete with fallacy dialogues, occur when Socrates chucks his egotistical
toys, and returns to divine or semi-divine "revelations."

Aristotle however clenched the matter, and held up human enlighten-
ment for let us say 2000 years. The poisoned gumdrop of the syllogism
was sweet in the human mouth; it dispensed with the need of direct
observation. It was easier to work on a mono-theistical dogmatic basis
than on manifest nature. In fact manifest nature has never submitted.

Science at last wriggles out. Language, literature still bears the marks
of the centuries of oppression. Thought goes on, the thinking biologist
KNOWS a great deal that escapes syllogistic statement. Literature tagging
on, now, I mean within the last few years, begins to struggle against the
forms of the formulae.

I don't know how to stress the matter. Simple as these things are
they are extremely difficult to convey even to the intelligent members
of the community, and by that I do not mean the writers of pseudo-
philosophic essays (so called); I mean even the better literati. I once
spent several hours getting into (at least for the time then being) the
head of a most distinguished contemporary that my not being a Chris-

tian did NOT mean that I was a Protestant and not a Catholic. For twenty years he had been arguing Catholicism against Protestantism.

After dealing with another, also renowned author, and finally getting into his head that by Greek polytheism I mean the twelve divinities of the Homeric saga, he finally gasped: "Why, almost nobody believes in that."

Gentle reader, are these things answers?

Gentle scientist, is it any more scientific to base your science on a final impossibility or antinomy or fallacy, or to admit SEVERAL components in your ignotum?

As to the evils of monism, and its consequent uniforms, uniformities, etc., it is, apart from the individual case, bad sociology, you can NOT in a healthy state have everyone complying with one set of rules as if impelled by one set of motives.

After all, the Roman empire showed some common sense on at least several occasions; and one of the most notable signs of that common sense was in allowing people of similar temperament (even if excessive) to concentrate on one particular cult, or on several cults, which were THEIR cult or cults, and not the cult of the whole populum.

The advantage of a cult over a vague bohemia is that the cult does not require the continuous production of sham art, by people who only do it as an excuse to escape from the horrors of bourgeois existence, life of the post-Victorian or other small town family, etc.

As to the minor advantages, the superiority of the temple over the museum, etc., the reader can make these applications for himself.

In this note I am out merely to combat a fundamental error, a fundamental shallowness of all European and American thought often not even "thought" or an uniform silly assumption.

The race has produced nothing better, naturally one "can't go back to"; whatever we imagine as a Hellenic religion won't be anything the Greek or Latin would have recognized, but that is of no importance.

The opponents might do worse than study the subject before deciding in the negative. It is not a case of believing something, but of having certain ideas in the mind.

The virtue of the myths is that one does not have to believe them. The virtue of the myths is that no one can use Leda or Daphne in a revival meeting.

Before Socrates were the sages, and they let these matters alone. The one intelligent ethical teacher, Confucius, also let these matters ALONE.

The modern world is offered the dry biscuits of let us say Shaw, an utter ignoramus, or of other similar know-nothings that have never thought about any THING whatsoever. I mean just that: any *thing;* they pass on second-hand ideas, they subject them to "logical treatment," that is to say they compose them and decompose them and rejoin fragments of them without ever tackling the *fonds.* They don't even get as far as an enlightened Mediaeval theologian. After all Richard St. Victor did think. Or at any rate he did envisage some form of mental activity not reducible to syllogistic formulation.

The Catholic church maintained its life, perhaps only so long as it maintained its polytheistic assumptions.

But in times of stress man has, or a few more intelligent men have cried out for "gods." Gemisto with a definite reason, with a localized immediate objective, and possibly because of its localization and immediacy advocated a reinstatement, but in so far as his gods emerge from one (Neptune) he is not a fundamental polytheist.

One can not place the urge in anything so unimportant or trivial as a desire to maintain the Greek empire and keep Turks out of Constantinople. Argument along these lines was possibly the only way to bring the matter to the attention of a Byzantine emperor, but it has no philosophical weight.

Our modern oppression, dilemma, embarrassment, great pit, desolation etc. is more profound. The spirit of man hath not where to hang its hat. The constellations find no convenient park-bench to repose on.

As the GREAT theory or revelation, the intelligentzia is reduced not to philosophy but to a system for curing lunatics, meaning Mr. Freud's pathology. Which is no place to take a child, and is no real substitute for Acis and Galatea, certainly no ersatz for Syrinx.

There are certain fundamental confusions, certain clichés of association dating from the Semitic ingerence. It remains that the great Hellenic myth, the body and complex of that myth, not of one inventor not dead with the Greeks, but alive certainly in the time of Augustus, not as faith, (for heaven's sake let us chuck out these mind-clots faith and belief as if they were essentials to life).

Not as faith but as a mode of approach, as a modality of comprehending the universe, are the great heritage. They are the great invention, and in them is the wisdom.

Confucius, finding perhaps a similar beauty in Chinese legend, ordered the wise to respect the RITES. Not a word about belief in verbal formulations.

For temporary reasons, for limited objectives it may at times be advisable to emphasize, even to over-emphasize the need of some "moral" factors, loving-kindness.

But superficial and temporary sociological, or merely political reasons can not with impunity be confused with philosophic or psychological reasons.

What we have now is a mass of human young exposed on the barren hillside; they have no decent mental furnishings, rationalism, Freud, Christian junk of the worst Christian periods, devoid of even the mediaeval Christian picturesqueness; in fact no decent scaffoldings of any kind, no decent circle of reference for any experience whatsoever. The mind needs such scaffoldings, not as fact, but as some sort of scale of comparison.

The Semitic tradition breeds nothing but zeals, intemperate phobias, servants of the lord, etc., lopsided, bungling.

The whole of the modern mechanism "religious," i.e. monotheist or rationalist, gives no vocabulary; or at least it gives a silly impoverished list of words inadequate for a Cook's tourist: how much, too much, which way to the railway station. One hundred phrases for the tritest occasions.

There are some forms of assumption and prejudice so set that one doesn't know where to attack them. To yell with full lungs, to jab a gun in the fellow's ribs, to smack it down with double-sized capitals.

THESE NUMBSKULLS ARE NOT THINKERS; the whole of the Occident has been bluffed for centuries. I mean that the whole of western philosophy for centuries is based on the puny assumption of monism, or monotheism. This hypothesis is not treated as a tentative hypothesis, but professedly or half-consciously underlying the whole of so called philosophic writing is this trivial and unsupported and unsupportable assumption of oneness.

It is there as a mental convenience. It is difficult for these half-glanded verbalists to conceive a polytheistical or a polysic universe.

When they do enter argument they assume that the ONLY alternative to a monism is a dualism, and they parrot a classroom tag that "that is a dualism and impossible."

A dualism is not perhaps impossible, but it is wholly uninteresting, and as a bit of mental furnishing it gives, or tends to give merely a god and devil, an indigent and silly cosmos; no better than that of Salem. In fact a good deal of the worst Christianity is dualism, and a very poor form at that.

In accordance as a man is intelligent, he seeks after gods. The pest of "faith" or "belief" is another Semitic intemperance.

[Catholicism] (c. 1940)

I am against the individual components of whatever gang or ganglion or unsewn category of persons support the international usury racket or who impede the light regarding workings of [the] same. Captan's annonam! By whatever mechanism, by whatever monopolism, by whatever racket, gold-hog or bank-hog at 60% supernescheck.

It is permitted that a man WORK at clarifying his own ideas. I have been asked whether I am a Catholic and I am not ready to deny it. I don't expect any organization to accept responsibility for my speculations. I do not 13th March anno XVIII deny any Catholic dogma.

As I see it the theologians of the Church did during at least one thousand years try honestly to work out an exposition of truth, they were often bigoted.

Such hilarity, says of Scotus Erigena. Yet the heretics were, so far as I have yet managed to make it, always wrong. The heretical parts of Erigena are errors *teste meo*. These men with illegible manuscripts, no clear printed page were burdened, were smothered, were hogswoggled by the scriptures. They think with light. *Omnia quae sunt, lumina sunt.* Their minds function O.K. chief, and then they try to square what they know with some damned idiocy taken out of the barbarian writings and the result is a gormy mess. When they run straight, they end up on Plato or Aristotle and cite Greek authorities. I am for a Confucian treatment of the Christian religion, which of course wouldn't leave your Anglican archbishops pissing room in a latrine.

The Church, servant of Rothschild, is certainly not a Christian organization, the lackey and pet boy of usuriocracy is not a religion, it is a bordello and not clean as a bordello.

29

The sixty-eight points of the American Catholic Bishops are pretty good. I recommend them for active consideration.

The degeneration of the wheat cult into a Metro-Goldwyn film? Two thousand years of progressive ignorance?

All very embarrassing just now, when the American Catholic Bishops have come clean, and blasted brother Possum's Episcopalian inactivity and the doctrine that the Church should never play the man.

Just as I am about ready to accept the mass and the Holy Communion, neither of which is Semitic in origin (on condition that the mass remain in Latin, unless it can be chanted in Greek or Chinese or some idiom whereto that no bleating subsidized cleric can pretend comprehension). Here comes friend Every to remind us that good old Achilles was born Ratti. The cardinals used to call old Ratti, in private, that damned Jew from Milan.

At any rate one can whole-heartedly spit of Jehovah, and Chang-Ti is as good a name as another. The Jewish conception of a maniacal sadist ruling all things is NOT a necessary component of thought. A bridal djin of most unpleasant and savage tendencies is not even the god of Dante, and the Church was the adversary of Judah during its non-usurious (or at any rate theoretically non-usurious) epoch.

The simple world of nymphs and satyrs is not the only alternative to a crazy quilt of abstracter superstitions. Brother Every offers a false dilemma. I deny, at any rate tentatively, that we believe anything non-European. The ethics of Confucius and Mencius coincide with a good deal that the European or his transplants can accept. I haven't yet found anything better and I [am] not ready to offer a philosophical system. I suspect I shall be found in the end with the religious.

Catholicism is a Mediterranean not a Palestinian construction. It is burdened with the lousy Old Testament, the survival of which is a powerful testimony to the spell of turgid rhetoric over barbarians, with good old rousing up-cock-and-at-'em and what-a-gal-to-bed-with

> Bin schwartz und dock bin Schon
> Ihr Tochter von Ierusalem

swank sex and the rest of it, without which Ezekiel could have eaten his dung in quiet and been tucked under the temple ruins.

I have unfortunately been unable to find any serious polytheism in printed or manuscript tradition; nevertheless the monotheists are lazy. It is easier to think of one god than of five. The Church (meaning the Catholic, all too Catholic perhaps, and Roman, perhaps insufficiently, yes, surely insufficiently Roman) made a sage compromise, and the Trinity is less devastatingly deleterious to manners and conduct than the *monos*. Monotheism spells fanaticism and the messing of hierarchy.

> *Semen est verbum Dei.*

I deny quite flatly that all faith is dead. There is a *mysterium* and no rain of cosmic atoms, or "rays" as the fashionable term is among the illiterate (variety column in the second weeklies, current science in the American Supplements) has obliterated one scrap of the mystery.

Also let us keep our minds clear, and not flop into the H. G. Wellsian era when false dilemma lay in every bordello. It is possible to damn *semitism* without beating up Z, F, L, and R. Only from Jan. 1st, 1940 (XVIII) it is *verboten* to damn any -*ism* without first defining it.

I think further.

What they got unconsciously, the taken for granted part of Christianity probably owes more to the Stoic than to all other sources lumped together, both the ethic and cosmic scheme. I suggest that analysis of belief will show more even in the general mixed bag is due to Cicero (or to what he summarized) than to all that can be dragged out of the lawn prophets' erotica and snotty pessimism of the Old Testament; which is after all a collection of heterogeneous matter, parts of which have rhetorical value, and parts of which are arrogant and conceited tushery. The Biblical apologists are not as a rule men who have read much else, or who have returned calmly to Bible-fugging AFTER familiarity with civil writing of either Greeks, Romans or extreme Orientals.

I have for years tried to keep off religious discussion, believing certain things unknowable or at least unascertained and therefore not subject to satisfactory verbal explanation. I have no objection to any man's religiously backing his own intuition or Anschauung, but if a man or group pretend to rationality, I strongly object to blatantly defective reasoning.

I have never met any real fundamental polytheism in my historical research. At best I have found an initial monism or monotheos with a lot of descendents. But the concept of fundamental polytheism is not an intellectual impossibility. I am not proclaiming a religion, I am asserting a fact. The concept is possible, any system of reasoning about the cosmos as if the said concept could not exist is defective. It is *one* of possible concepts, and must be eliminated before any system can claim perfect rationality.

Apart ça, you have dogmatic religions. The burblings of writers who treat religion without sound reason and without any historic knowledge of the religions they claim to believe are, so far as I am concerned, unworthy of specific attention.

A statement of belief in abstract terms which lack even the discipline of mediaeval scholasticism can not, I think, very greatly matter. In asserting the ideogramic method as the sole satisfactory method for our time, I do not abrogate the known criteria of logic *for logicians*. A man acting in that restricted field must at least accept its criteria.

The Organum According to Tsze sze (1942)

Confucius is the greatest social philosopher that ever lived. The great Chinese dynasties, those that lasted 3 centuries were founded on the rules of Confucius. When China has been well governed it has been according to Confucian teaching.

My American version of his Ethics with the title, the *Great Learning* was published by Glen Hughes in 1928 in the Washington University Graphika, and has gone in various further editions in England and America. That version was made before I knew enough about ideogram and when I erroneously supposed that Pauthier, Legge and co. had understood the original text. I have been discontented with the version for some time, missing out some of the high spots, although it contains the main sense of the original, and as I mentioned last time, I have now brought out a bilingual edition, Chinese and Italian in collaboration with the avv. Alberto Lucchini, having analyzed every ideogram, and I believe set forth the true meaning on examination of the text of the Organum, I find that Pauthier and Legge have not produced a satisfactory interpretation. Legge, tremendously learned, his book a treasure, had read commentaries, or at least copied some Chinese who had, but he seems never to have LOOKED, really looked at an ideogram. I am now going to read a new version. It may be hard to follow, but it is my only way to publish it in English while the war is on. You will have to listen carefully, because the sense is deep.

The Organum is Confucian teaching, contained in the 21st chapter of the Choung Young: and the 5 chapters that follow, in form of comment on 21st chap./ the tradition was oral till Tsze Sze wrote it down in this form. It is philosophy in the wide sense, whereas the *Great Learning* is more strictly Ethics (expressed) and philosophy implied. The form is similar in that the *Great Learning* consists of 7 pp. of Kung's testament, followed by Tsang's commentary. I call this piece Organum so that the hearer will compare it with Bacon's *Organum*. You might watch for two themes that run thru the pattern. One that the fittest or most important study of it is man, secondly that there is a uniform process in nature, that is a basis, an unvarying norm (that's what Choung Young means) unwobbling norm in nature; a basis for science, and foresight. Confucius was born 551 B.C. and died B.C. 479. Cf./ this organum, with, let us say Arnold's condensation of Spinoza, and you will find, I think, all the difference between something that hits a target—Organum—and something that just narrowly misses.

Appendix

To Douglas C. Fox
23 Febbraio ['35]

Dear FOX.

The more I think about that damn pamphlet the more it worries me.

Frob/DID condence in Paideuma/bloody nuissance that isn't pubd/in English.

I am sending you proof of the Fenollosa/far from ideal presentation/

Fen/ composed it as a lecture. I cut out unnecessary words/nevertheless it does cohere and cover a BASE.

My How to Read/ and ABC of Reading also cohere.

It is one thing to do catchy magazine articles, and another to GET THE POINTED end of the wedge in 32 pages.

An ideogram of ESSENTIALS of Frob's/ thought. Introd. by Fox, and the rest in condensed CONCRETE cases illustrative.

Cd/ use my two or three pages of the drum telegraph. The legends and stories are too easy going and long.

HELL. I know what is needed BUT damn it I cant take six months off to do it.
Wonder if Frob/ himself KNOWS how to put the ESSENTIAL bases of what he thinks into such telegraphic form.
Lemme see wot I can do off me yown bat/

1. Form of objects is DUE to CAUSES
(this kicks the pants off all the anglo/shit/xon muddle and lousy indifference to art
2. teacher an ASS not to see that child not stupid asking if the T was the tail of the caT.
3. spatial and temporal/ in and out cultures.
(I might putt it cuntal and spermatozoic civilizations).
4. art in material
     vs/
arab botanist, all in his head and to hell with kettles and pots.
5. traces of high civilization (as in drum telegraph and language of (not exactly melody but at least thematic material as vocabulary).
《nothing is without efficient cause.》

whether one can get more than this at the thin end of wedge I duuno.

IF this much cd' be illustrated by the Geheimrat's own words/ paragraph from here and pp/ frum thaaaar,
it wd. help toward proper Eng/ editions at least of Paideuma and the less discursive work reports of expeditions etc. meandering about
and to hell with Spengler/ that ought to [be] got over somehow.

or getting thru ANG/ sex crust or layer of baby fat and suet

better begin with OBJECTIVE and concrete data/ leaving the imminence and mystic aura etc. to later typographic manifestations.

That don't exclude the memory of LIVING men as evidence. That you have touched in the Advocate article/ paesant legend as document, thass O.K.

In fact that ought to be in the summary (BUT Frazer etc.) perhaps a line to distinguish the advance made by Frob. if it can be clearly and briefly stated.

How far can the Geheimrat be bother[ed] with the proposition. It is a chance of ESTABLISHING his position in several countries. COULD be his most important essay if he can interrupt his actual work to do it. I know what a damn bore it sometimes is to be asked to restate what one has lived with for years, when one is in process of LIVING something new. Read him out this anyhow.

If Ogden weren't such an ass, he wd' WANT this stuff for Psyche, but I suppose his INFANTILISM insists on being largest frog in his own puddle. He DID a damn good essay on Bacon (I must admit that and in a country where there is NO serious thought, he hath virtue.)

yrz EZ P

To Douglas C. Fox
[19]37 [30 feb.]

Dear Fox

I cd/ advertise the Afrikaarchiv a bit in present book. If anybody has taken down SPECIMENS of the actual drum telegraph language or the flute tune language.

Might just as well publicize Frankfurt as publicize Levy-Bruhl. Anyhow it is the music languages I want/ whether they arise from association (to what %) or morse alphabet, or mixture, how far time, how far pitch, how far mere signal code (secret or other).

Can't use very much, I mean it can't fill an awful lot of space but might be edge of wedgeish.

Mebbe there is something already in print.

The Makute stuff wd/ also introduce to different circle.

I have already said I recd/ the information. But it didn't have any FURTHER implication as it was sent to me.

Whether a racial infiltration? or a geographic area.

Also the Mohamedan anti-usury trend MIGHT open up vein.

and so forth.

Editor's Note: This letter has to be considered in relation to Pound's attempt to establish whether primitive peoples who use musical languages or various other types of nonverbal communication practice usury or not. Fox's response of 2 March 1937, although generic on language, confirms for Pound that natural people do not practice usury: "Generally, without knowing much about it, I would say that usury was an attribute solely of the so-called Hochkulturen, that is, it plays no role in the economic life of the Naturfolker" (BRBL, Folder "Frobenius Institute," 599).

Happy New Yrea

          Still using Schwegler / must say he seems very
same as far as my knowledge covers matter he mentions.

DesCartes' mind seems MORE like a pea rattling in bladder ,whenever
he gets off mathematics(where I believe he made greatest invention
ever).

Spinoza (as have always, or for 30 years believed) rather better
BUT. no proof of unity; i;e; no PROOF there is only ONE
substance.

      I can accept " world as accident of divine substance "
that seems fair way of putting it; but does NOT imply that there
can be only ONE substance.

Even with his two attributes matter (extention) and thought; dont
necessitate onlyONE substance or nonethoes. cd/ be 5 or 7

substances from all of which one cd. abstract the two attributes
and leave the 5 or 7 or whatever number STILL mutually DIFFERENT

though meeting or affecting or having common ground in both thought
and matter.

          side diagram.

I still come back to old question I think I asked in Venice. Have you
ever met a proof of nones theos orxwhatever)/ or encountered

ANY serious polytheistc thought ANYwhere ? save possibly in these
presents ?

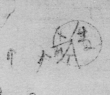

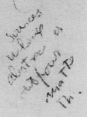

To George Santayana
2 Jan or 41

Happy New Year

Still using Schwegler / must say he seems very sane as far as my knowledge covers matter he mentions.

DesCartes' mind seems MORE like pea rattling in bladder, whenever he gets off mathematics (where I believe he made greatest invention ever).

Spinoza (as have always, or for 30 years believed) rather better BUT. no proof of unity; i.e., no PROOF there is only ONE substance.

I can accept "world as accident of divine substance" that seems fair way of putting it; but does NOT imply that there can be only ONE substance.

even with his two attributes matter (extention) and thought; dont necessitate only ONE substance or monotheos. cd/ be 5 or 7 substances from all of which one cd. abstract the two attributes and leave the 5 or 7 or whatever number STILL mutually DIFFERENT though meeting or affecting or having common ground in both thought and matter.

   vide diagram.
I still come back to old question I think I asked in Venice. Have you ever met a proof of monos (theos or whatever)/ or encountered ANY serious polytheiste thought ANYwhere ? save possibly in these presents?

Grand Hotel, Rome, 4, I, 1941

Dear E.P.   Aren't you wasting your time in looking for proofs? Proofs must rest either on tautology, because you have granted the conclusions in conceiving your premises, or on stupidity, because you are incapable of conceiving anything different from what happens to suggest itself. Mathematics and logic are tautological; any given essence has essential relations which are seen to be inevitable when once pointed out. Proofs there are therefore interesting because the[y] *deepen* apprehension; but they prove nothing about matters of fact. I don't know how you define "substance": Spinoza could prove that there was only one

Editor's Note: I include Santayana's letter of response to Pound as I found it in BRBL, Folder "Santayana, George," 1562.

substance because he conceived it as the *essence* and *truth* of all things lumped together. If there were two universes or two attributes the *true* universe and the *total* essence would evidently be the sum and system of those two universes and of those two attributes. But in calling this inevitable totality God or *Natura naturans*, he identified it with a dynamic unit or source; something not subject to proof or argument of any kind, but imported into the system by religious tradition or vitalistic myth.

I can't reply to your suggestions and diagrams because I don't understand them.

Existence comes in pulses, in strokes. I see no reason for not stopping, or for stopping, anywhere in that flux. Existence has as many centres as it happens to have, as many moments[,] feelings, assumptions, questions—all in the air and with no power over one another. But if we have time and patience to study a *natural world*, posited as the source and common continuum in all this existence, we *assume* that it has dynamic unity: otherwise, from one point in it we could never justly infer or posit any other point in it. This is my argument for materialism.

G.S.

Pragmatic Aesthetics

Pragmatic Aesthetics of E.P.
(c. 1940–1943)

Pound did not write a "Treatise on Aesthetics," nihilominus, there exists an aesthetic system, coherent, not born perfect and completed in 1910 but developing continually and coherently from the early attempt, "Prolegomena" in three pages; and "The Serious Artist," *Poetry Review*, London, 1912, 1913, to "How to Read," 1929, to the present. Point of view very different from Croce's point of view.

Writings by the poet, letters to G.S., conversations with G.S.

PRAGMATIC AESTHETICS

Source
Pound had forgotten the phrase "vital nutrimento," Dante cited by G. Saviotti, "Pensiero estetico e il gusto," p.7

but one finds parallel in
"How to Read"
"nourishing it with the food of impulse," etc.
Indice, 20 March 1930
He accepts *almost* the Dantesque position (mutatis mutandis)
NOT of course for medieval Christianity; but for the relation of "truth" to "art." He dislikes the phrase "beautiful *lie*."
Personally he is not interested in fiction but in truth.
This is a personal and autobiographical matter, not a theoretical one. The theoretical has to be separate from what is personal.
Private Letter

A Dantesque idea never lost in his mind
"that melody which most concentrates the soul in itself." Futile, almost harmful. An "aesthetics" that wants to define good art and bad art, high and low, with a single formula.

E.P. Pragmatic Aesthetics
   which *FUNCTIONS.*
I.   To nurture the discrimination, the judgment, to predict the contemporary works that will outrun time, like race-horses.
II.   And to stimulate the artists' production and improve the works *to be done.*

Stages:
   period of meditation; age 15 to 22, no manuscript remains. 300 sonnets destroyed, etc. mysticism, discontent with verbal display.
   reading of Dante: study of 10 languages

Rodolphi Agricolae   Phrisii, De Inventione Dialectica.
   always leaves him discontent with the indefinite contemporary *terminology* and the terminology after the Renaissance.

And also with the terminology of George Santayana of five years ago.

One must not define the gun as if it were the explosion, or the gun barrel, or the bullet, etc.
   24 parts of a scholastic definition.
He insists: loss of the sense of terminology almost from the moment when they begin to look at things (that is, to look more at (something other) than terminology), a progress, YES, but with this progress there came a loss.

"Thomas Aquinas is not a serious character" (*New Review,* January, 1931)

"Paradosso" (*Corriere Emiliano,* 1930). NO. He hates paradox, a frivolous mode, he hates this joke, trying to be amusing;
   He loves the strong declaration; but he considers the violence "even of speech" an error because it is less effective than the exact word (error because it produces a reaction).

Stages.

Early manifestoes, empirical.

Dont's ("Poetry," 1913) (*Fiea Letteraria*, translation 1929)

Vortex. Blast. 1914

Vorticism. Fortnightly Review. July 1914.

    paragraph on *Vortex*, elaborated. *Instigations*, 1920.

    "How to Read," 1929.

        phanopoeia

        melopoeia

        logopoeia

History/

    Impressionism. revivifying sense of color in painting.

    "Aesthetic" period 1880–1900, up to Debussy

melange, interpenetration; osmosis of the arts: *defining an art in the terminology of others.* 1880–1910.

      \versus\

    seeking to define each art

in the terminology of *that* art itself.

PART II

The form of thinking, or "HOW TO THINK."

utility of the general formula, negligible.

    The Spirit of Romance, 1910, Preface.

"Critical formulas are points of departure, NOT circumscriptions, not 'laws' for future artists."

Attack against abstraction.

    FENOLLOSA *The Chinese Written Language*

See: development.   four senses of the Divina Commedia.

    literal, allegorical, anagogical, moral;

        Letter to Can Grande

cf/ Vorticism, *Fortnightly Review*, 1914.

    mathematics,   the writing

    arithmetic

algebraic

geometric

analytic.

PPS/ To Fenollosa *fundamental.*
That the same formula serves the same man at two different epochs different for contents is THE CONDEMNATION of the abstract formula.
(Cited as private letter to G.S.)
The point is not to agree or disagree but to show E.P. point of view.

[The] true science, true thinking is ideogrammic in the sense that the general is composed of *definite particulars known directly* by the thinker.

Art is the particular declaration that *implies* the general; and being particular (Hamlet, Odysseus, Madame Bovary) may not divert, distract, melt and muddle like an abstract declaration which becomes a party cry; or cloak or mask for a hundred different ideas.

Not intending to write abstract things, there remains, however, half a million words in the "Prolegomena," written in different crises in order to defend contemporary writers and artists, "like conversation" "notes to serve the history of the epoch, etc." but not made primarily for this, made for the moment of the crisis; to have the particular work prevail, to make possible the food for the artist's life, for the individual, to stimulate American productivity and to improve it.
    EVERYTHING to make the art and the artist function, grow, create.

Proportion/ H.H. wants other essays like "Horace." A note that Pound had recast and left 10 years in London; and which he considers "dead" because it does not lead to production.
        (conversations with the poet)

The characteristic of the classic is not the formal exterior; it is the "eternal freshness."

Contrast of the classifications (categories) in "How to Read" with the *Poetics* of Aristotle (which is a fragment, but perhaps Aristotle had not defined the categories of substance, only those of form that one finds in the *Poetics*).

Repeated tribute to the *Volgari Eloquio* in the published works of E.P.

His philosophy, for another essay. But certainly it is not lacking.

> NOTE: Prolegomena
> 500,000 remain, not the whole product but a selection
> And for 4 years he did not publish a word of prose, 1924–28.

> (beyond the quantity of personal letters).
> constipation? relative

Philosophy, philosophical expression [is] nothing but a vague fluid approximation; art achieves a MORE PRECISE manifestation.
Let. to G.S..
(hence the contradiction of Crocian hierarchy)

ref./ "How to Read"   "the setting of meaning," etc.

Different passages drawn from an issue of "Exile" edited by Pound in 1927.

A Note on the Texts

The manuscripts of *Machine Art and Other Writings* are preserved in BRBL. Each manuscript is typed with Pound's few handwritten corrections or additions. To avoid cluttering the text with editorial brackets, some of Pound's spelling or punctuation errors have been silently corrected, as have his frequent shorthand abbreviations.

Mostly undated in their original form, the texts are collected and reorganized in chronological order. The dates indicated at the beginning of texts are those written by Pound. Dates suggested by the archivists are bracketed. The titles are those given by Pound. The fragments are mostly untitled; some titles suggested by the archivists are inserted in brackets to distinguish them from Pound's titles.

Machine Art is preserved in the folder "Machine Art," 3820. The text is typed and occupies the thirty-three numbered folios; page 34–35 contains a list of photographs. The date as indicated by Pound is 1927, corrected by hand in 1930. The text, in fact, is the revised version of one originally written in 1927, whose carbon copy is contained in folder 3821. Pound's handwritten corrections appear throughout the text. An important revision is made at pp. 5 and 6, and another at p. 10 with the insertion of a new page numbered 10a. *Pound e la scienza* included the text dated 1927.

How to Write is preserved in the folder "Collected Prose," 2940, and it is the sole content of the folder. The date 1930 is indicated by Pound on pages 90 and 103. A thick brown paper in the folder in Pound's hand indicates its content as "E[zra]/P[ound] Varia." The typed text appears to be an unfinished fragment and occupies thirty-nine pages, partially numbered with interleaved carbon copy pages. Some interleaved and untyped pages contain Pound's minor annotations. The last page of the folder contains a copy of a fragment which starts with "The fault of Russell . . . ." This fragment is also contained in another folder (No. 2939) as part of "Them 'Eavy Thinkers," and in this form it is edited here.

Under the title *Addenda* I collect nineteen mostly untitled and undated fragments which appear to belong to the late 1920s and the 1930s. Some of them were written by Pound at the end of the 1920s to connect the various sections of his planned twelve-volume edition of *Collected Prose* (Gallup, *A Bibliography*, 452, and my n. 6 above), and in fact most of them are preserved in the folders "Collected Prose." The title *Addenda* is given by Pound only to the first three fragments collected here. They are preserved in the folder "Collected Prose, mainly from 'New Age,'" 2938. The other fragments, in the order of their appearance, are preserved in the following folders: "Collected Prose, mainly from 'New Age,'" 2938; "Appunti," 2258 (originally in Italian); "Fragments," 5278; "Unidentified Fragments," 5277; "Notes," 5301; "Notes," 5301; "Collected Prose," 2934. *Them 'Eavy Thinkers* is in "Collected Prose," 2939. Of the six following fragments, the first four are contained in "Collected Prose," 2945; the two others are contained in "Philosophy and Religion," 4188, and in "Aristotle NOTES ON," 2266. *Honesty of the word does not permit dishonesty of the matter* is in "Collected Prose, 1934–1935," 2943. *Value of Style* is in "Collected Prose," 2938.

The texts are all typed; some of them contain Pound's handwritten corrections. The fragment, which I have indicated as preserved in the folder "Aristotle NOTES ON," 2266, could have been written during Pound's reading of Aristotle's *Nicomachaean Ethics*, since another fragment clearly related to that reading (*Pound e la scienza*, 222) is preserved in the folder. I therefore suggest for it the date 1935–1936.

A Problem of (Specifically) Style was published by Pound in "New English Weekly," VI, vi, 22 Nov. 1934, 127–128.

Ogden and Debabelization was published in "New English Weekly," VI, 20, 28 Feb. 1935, 410–411. The latter two texts were included in *Ezra Pound e la scienza* (1987) and are now collected in *Ezra Pound: Poetry and Prose Contributions to Periodicals*, 10 volumes, prefaced and arranged by Lea Baechler, A. Walton Litz, and James Longenbach (New York and London: Garland, 1991), 6: 14–15 and 251–252.

European Paideuma is preserved in the folder "European Paideuma," 3323. The date 1940, handwritten in the right margin of the first page near the title, appears to be in D. C. Fox's hand. The typed text occupies six folios. The title "European Paideuma by Ezra Pound" was followed by "edited by Douglas C. Fox," which was crossed out. The text has no corrections or additions. It appears to be a revised version of a primitive draft written in 1939, contained in the same folder, and dated "7 August." According to Pound's correspondence with Fox, preserved in the Beinecke among the correspondence with the Frobenius Institute, Folders 596–601, the English version of *European Paideuma* would have been published in the review "German and You," while Fox planned to translate it into German. One letter from Fox to Pound dated 8 Sept. 1939 and containing a series of questions on the text shows that Pound's *European Paideuma* appeared to be mostly incomprehensible to Fox, who asked Pound to revise the text. The version I publish appears to be the revised version. However, the text was not published. I publish *European Paideuma* in its entirety, with the exception of a few lines which I judge to be superfluous. Some excerpts of *European Paideuma* were published by Charles Norman in his *Ezra Pound* (New York: Macmillan, 1960). See Gallup 183–184. *European Paideuma* was also included in *Ezra Pound e la scienza*.

Convenit esse Deos is contained in the folder "Convenit esse Deos," 3133. The text is an undated fragment and does not contain Pound's additions or corrections. The central topic of the text, also present in Pound's correspondence of the early 1940s with George Santayana, in *European Paideuma* and [*Catholicism*], persuades me to situate it in the same period, that is, 1940–1942. *Convenit esse Deos* occupies eight folios, partially numbered. The third folio is typed on Pound's personal stationery:

"Ezra Pound   res publica, the public convenience.
                 Rapallo, via Marsala 12, int. 5."

Under the title [*Catholicism*], I collect three untitled fragments. Two of these are preserved in the folder "Catholicism," 2811. At the top of the second fragment's page, the date "1940," which appears to be in Fox's hand, suggests that this fragment was part of the "European Paideuma" project. The third is contained in the folder "Religion," 4894. The only date which I found in them, "Jan. 1st 1940 (XVIII)," is indicated in the text by Pound himself. The typed fragments occupy six folios with a large empty space. At the top of the first fragment is a handwritten note by Pound "not sent!" There are no additions, and one minor correction is on the third fragment.

"The Organum According to Tsze sze" is the text of a radio speech contained in the folder "Radio N.82, Confucianum Organum, 17–18 August 1942," 4487. The text is typed on a large-size folio with Pound's handwritten corrections. On the lower-right margin, a handwritten addition "5-7-45 Rapallo," not in Pound's hand, marks the date of confiscation by the U.S. military from the poet's apartment of material assumed to be incriminating.

Two Letters to D. C. Fox, preserved in the order in which they appear, are in the folders "Frobenius Institute 1934–1935," 597, and "Frobenius Institute 1937," 599. The first one occupies three folios, and the date " '35" appears to be in Pound's handwriting. The second occupies one folio; the date " '37" appears to be in Pound's hand.

"The Organum According to Tsze sze" and "Two Letters to D.C. Fox" were included in *Ezra Pound e la scienza*.

A Letter to George Santayana is contained in the folder "Santayana, George," 1562. The date "January 2," is by Pound, the letter is from 1941, as is evident from Santayana's response of 1 April 1941. The letter contains an undeciphered addition and one diagram. I include the facsimile of the letter among the illustrations.

Pragmatic Aesthetics of E.P. is an undated typed text originally in Italian, whose title is *Estetica Pragmatica di E.P.* It is preserved in the folder "Estetica pragmatica," 3317. The text occupies nine folios. Pound's additions are in red ink, with the exception of the following, handwritten in black ink on the left side of the first page: "ho bisogno di una serie compiuta dell'Indice e di 2 copie di Mystere Cocteau" [I need a complete series of *Indice* and two copies of *Mystère Cocteau*]. The text also contains pencil corrections and additions not in Pound's hand. Mary de Rachewiltz suggests that these could be by G. B. Vicari and that the text might have been included in Vicari's editions of *Biblioteca minima*, in which *Carta da visita* was published in 1942. The handwritten indication (not in Pound's hand) of the typographical size of the word "FUNCTIONS" as "2[m]m" confirms that the text was intended for publication. I suggest for *Estetica Pragmatica* the date 1940 to 1943. Because of continual references to "G.S." in the text, *Pragmatic Aesthetics* has in fact to be located in the Italian years of Pound's friendship and correspondence with Santayana. According to the archive, this correspondence began in 1939 with a letter from Santayana from the Hotel Danieli (Venice) dated "30, XI, '39." In *Pragmatic Aesthetics* Pound's bibliographical references are sometimes incorrect. Some errors have been silently corrected. Note also that the essay "The Serious Artist" was published in *Freewoman* in 1913.

A Note on the Illustrations

Machine Art contained a list of fifty illustrations occupying MS pp. 35 and 36. These photographs are preserved in BRBL, Folder "Photographs, Jan. 1976, Photos collected by Ezra Pound," which contains eighty-four photos, not all of which Pound planned to use. Other materials are preserved in Brunnenburg, probably among Homer Pound's correspondence, because of his assistance in collecting the illustrations for the planned edition of *Machine Art* (for the failure of this edition, see Gallup, *A Bibliography*, 449–450). The material preserved in Brunnenburg, when I compared it with the material in Beinecke, allows the possibility of reconstructing how Pound tries to express his viewpoint on machines. Pound's contribution to *The New Review* I:4 (Winter 1931–1932; issue on "Machines"), with fifteen photographs chosen, is among material preserved in BRBL. Material in Brunnenburg and in Beinecke shows that both Pound and his father requested the photos from American companies that were making machines in those years. The photographs collected pertain not only to the machine as motor parts or mechanism, but to precision instruments such as recording pyrometers, telescopes, and telescopic devices. In addition, some fold-out photographs of landscapes with agricultural products show Pound's idea of perceiving in the machine the way of improving the production of nature. This appears in Pound's interest in agricultural machines in *Machine Art*.

Donald Gallup, informing us (*A Bibliography*, 449–450) about Pound's long search in collecting the photographic material, confirms the importance that Pound attributed to the illustrations. Pound's list appears to be mostly provisional. He organized the materials in nine sections, each section containing machines of different types, made by different companies. Some photos preserved in the Yale Archive have numbers written on their backs in blue or red pencil. The blue numeration appears to organize the order of illustrations for the planned illustration of *Machine Art* (1927–1930), while the red pencil markings seem to organize the sequence for the special issue of *The New Review* (Winter 1931–1932) devoted to machines, in which Pound included only fifteen of the photos previously collected. Crucial in my attempt to reconstruct the photographs that Pound planned to include in *Machine Art* have been materials in Brunnenburg, mostly publicity brochures containing detailed technical descriptions of individual machines. Along with a selection of twenty-six photos, I also include in the section "Other Illustrations" three pictures contained in the Yale and Brunnenburg materials which show Pound's idea of connecting machine and nature. The twenty-six photos I include do not document the entire sections indicated by Pound, because it has been impossible to precisely reconstruct Pound's planned sequence.

The first section (photos 1–13) is mostly lacunae. I did not find in Brunnenburg any brochure of William Sellers and Co. Following Pound's indication ("Mostly pieces of a 'Drill Grinder' showing the formal elements in the machine"), I include here photos that show mostly formal elements of machines, although they do not depict drill-grinders.

Photos 14–15, from Warren Knight, are those indicated by Pound "Pieces of Sterling precision transit, not strictly a machine." The brochure in Brunnenburg explains photo 15 as the telescope known as "Sterling Precision Transit, Philadelphia Model No. 2-b," and photo 14 as "Wye Bearing on which cylindrical shaped pivots of the telescope axle rest . . . and eliminates uncertainty."

Photo 16, from Orton and Steinbrenner, is described in the brochure as "Type No. 8. Wheel steam of Coal Handling equipment displacing the cost of 20 men." Pound's choice shows that his interest in machines was strongly related to matters of economy.

Photos 17–18 are described in the brochure of the Wellman-Seaver-Morgan Co. Illustration no. 17 reproduces the brochure's fourth page, and it is evident that Pound primarily sees in it machine dynamics as the result of applied forces and controlled strains. Photo 18, as described on the bulletin's first page, was "the great 250-ton revolving crane mounted on the hull of the old Battleship Kearsarge Crane, officially known as the U.S. Navy Crane Ship No. 1." Pound indicates them as "cranes, the kearsage, or gothic."

Photos 19–21 show Pound's interest in the recording pyrometer. Photo 19 is described in the brochure of the Brown Company as "a new single recording pyrometer used where a record of the temperature at only one point is required. . . . A single strong purple record line is made on a 7″ chart and the instrument incorporates a ribbon shift mechanism which discloses the past impression on the chart immediately after it has been made"; that is, a kind of mechanical instrument that measures the temperatures in relation to time. Writing is therefore the recording of a measurable function of physics. Photo 20 is described in the same brochure as a "Multiple Record Recorder. This instrument makes 1, 2, 3, 4, or 6 records in distinctive color markings. . . . A dial numbered and colored to correspond with the record lines indicates the active thermocouple." Photo 21 is described in the brochure as "support permit[ting] writing on chart. The chart is indicated with driving roll and platen so that notes can be made in ink or pencil."

Photo 22, Shepard Cranes and Electrical Hoist, indicates Pound's consideration of machines in terms of economy. The following description was attached to photo 22 in a hand other than Pound's: "These machines load bags of sugar into barges. A mechanical handling installation of this type in a country where common labor is so cheap (Japan) demonstrates its great economy."

Photo 23 is from a New York company, Hayward. This photo, which Pound also selected for *The New Review*, relates machines to the improvement of nature's productivity. According to the attached description, not in Pound's hand, the machine is handling acid phosphate in a fertilizing plant.

Photos 24–26 are indicated by Pound as "Bliss presses." The preserved section of the brochure emphasizes precision and high-power production. Photo 25 "shows an operator on a 'Bliss' No. 21 press blanking, forming and piecing bicycle bell bases at the rate of 13,000 per 10 hours." Photo 26 is described in the brochure as "showing intimately the production of automobile fenders in a plant equipped for contract work of this character."

Some of the photographs in this volume were reproduced in *The New Review*.

Photos 27–29. I include here three photographs preserved in the Beinecke Library and at Brunnenburg among *Machine Art* materials which show Pound's connecting of machine and nature, that is, the machine improving upon nature's powers. Pound seems to focus on the abundance of products of nature. Photo 27, is described as a wheat field in western Colorado; and photo 28 as a potato patch, East Mesa, Crystal River Valley. The descriptions are not in Pound's hand.

Other Illustrations

Photo 30. Facsimile of Pound's letter to Santayana, including diagram registering Pound's idea of a plural unity against the one of monotheism.

Photo 31. (p. xvi) Pound's drawing, contained in notes for *How to Read*, Folder 3598, shows "abstract" as reduction of the plural which is active in the language of primitive peoples ([Lévy-]"Bruhl") and in that of the Chinese ideogram ("Fenoll"[osa]).

Index

Ezra Pound is one of the most influential literary figures of
the twentieth century. His opinions and literary achievements
forcibly shaped the modernist movement. He is the author of
many familiar works, including *Personae, ABC of Reading,*
and *Cantos.*

Maria Luisa Ardizzone is Visiting Professor of Italian
Literature at New York University. Her writings include *Ezra
Pound e la Scienza.*

Library of Congress Cataloging-in-Publication Data
Pound, Ezra, 1885–1972.
Machine art and other writings : the lost thought of the Italian
years : essays / Ezra Pound ; selected and edited, and with an
introduction by Maria Luisa Ardizzone.

Includes
ISBN 0-8
ISBN 0-8
I. Ardizzo
PS3531.O
818'.520

DATE DUE
